Deep Space Dreaming

Loretta Laird

Published by **Rogue Phoenix Press**

Copyright © 2015

ISBN: 978-1-62420-165-3

Credits
Cover Artist: Designs by Ms G
Editor: Christie L. Kraemer

Prologue

Since the discovery of the light speed synthesizer, it had not taken humankind long to colonize their immediate galaxy and beyond. Within five generations, space travel was the norm and the floundering Earth was all but extinct.

One lone starship, which providence brought into Earth's orbit, contained the technology for such exploration. Little did the peace loving guardians, known as The Trinz, know of the race they had come to save. Earth's toxic atmosphere was no longer contained within its own galaxy. Pollution spread across the stars, across species and the insignificant rock just three planets from its star became the business of The Trinz. They came to help, driven by their compassionate souls from the far reaches of the universe to provide the means to escape the world dying from within. Humankind, unable to deviate from their intrinsic nature, began to spread, conquer and guzzle resources from world to world. Systematically, humans expanded into space feeding on every available resource.

Galaxy after galaxy was conquered and pillaged before the relentless force of human nature moved to the next prize. Metal stations under giant domes dominated planets draining their wealth and "civilizing" their species. Zones were created and space traffic monitored. Alpha Zone led into Bravo, before Charlie, Delta; the purge went on. Within a century, the human infestation was at breaking point. Races plotted against their foe, rebellions targeted ships and bases as death and war became rife and evolved into the norm. Human response to its own corruption was to plunge deeper into space, recruiting allies and acquiring wealth to fund the armies that pillaged the universe. Many species had united with the humans, too afraid of their might to refuse.

The Trinz tried to guide and mentor the primitive human race as they navigated the stars to no avail. Their arrogance proved too powerful. The Trinz retreated back to their own world, far from the reaches of the strange species so similar to themselves yet so primitive that it had inadvertently inflicted on the universe. They bided their time, awaiting the inevitable fall of the human race. Advanced in technology, their ability to travel through the power of the mind enabled them to reach a few good souls. Through dreams they managed to exert their influence. They met in a world called Killanti; mind within mind they whispered tales of an exotic paradise; tales of the old ways of how to live at one with all that surrounded them. These few fled from the chaos, guided to a new world to live in harmony with the universe. The rest stayed, living in the desolation humankind created. There they waited; praying for a miracle.

Chapter One

As her eyes opened and the early rays of the simulated daylight bombarded her senses, a cry of disappointment escaped Jenni's rosy, swollen lips. She reached up a hand and touched the tender flesh, feeling where the pressure of rough lips had assaulted them with desperate fervor as she bid a passionate farewell only moments prior. It seemed so real, her head throbbed where it struck a rock and her fingers gently explored the spot. Gasping Jenni felt the tender swell of the lump and recalled how she lost her footing on the rock. Her dream returned as it did each and every night. Yet this time it changed; this time he had been there. He revealed himself, no longer content to linger in the shadows of her mind.

It was a dream that haunted Jenni's every waking moment, pulling her back to blessed slumber each night. Her days were spent moving from task to task in a kind of trance, her mind elsewhere, thinking of the vivid dreams that were becoming more and more real.

Jenni's colleagues noticed a change in her in recent weeks. They commented on the way her pallid skin contrasted with the dark circles that rimmed her pale blue eyes. Their concern was touching to a girl who had no remaining family. Jenni, at the tender age of twenty three, was the youngest navigational pilot assigned to a seeker vessel. Her grades at the University of Holborn 4 had been exemplary. At her post on Chicago 3,

Jenni was in charge of navigation. Her role was to patrol and seek out rebels who may be harbored among the, thus far unchartered, planets of the Romeo Zone.

She was content with her lot. She loved to charter the planets and stars, marveling at the beauties of the universe. Jenni loathed the created atmospheres of the planetary domes. She longed for the freedom to explore a planet such as the one in her dreams where fresh air prevailed and greenery surrounded her. The feel of her bare feet on the soft, damp grass appeared to her as real as the constant presence that eluded her until last night. For last night, the bare chested man sought her out and made himself known to her.

The dreams started shortly after the tragic death of her parents. Jenni was eighteen. She had just begun her space pilot training and was awaiting her first leave. She planned to spend time with her parents on their home world of Texas 9, in the Lima Zone, when news of their demise reached her. Jenni's grief had been raw. Her tears fell relentlessly and none of her classmates could rouse her from her mourning. Sleep brought her only comfort as it blocked out the pain that ripped through her heart. At first, Jenni dreamed of a world cloaked in mist that swirled and moved in mysterious patterns around her. She sensed mountain ranges looming through the vapor, but no concrete images would form in her mind. Each wakening, she would try in vain to recreate the land she conjured in her dreaming. After many nights, hills and valleys had taken shape and Jenni felt a calmness that aided her sleep and refreshed her tired mind. Each night she would long for slumber to engulf her so she could escape from the metal world in which she resided to the landscapes of her dreams.

Time passed and the dream did not fade; rather the world grew around her. New life sprung up as flowers and streams appeared. Jenni was soon among the fragrant growth, strolling through gardens that seemed to be hers alone. Small flying creatures buzzed softly in her ear as gentle breezes caressed her face. The grass beneath her feet was as soft as the covers on her bed and she reveled in the sensation of sinking her toes into its lush pile.

The man appeared one night at the edges of her consciousness as if watching her wonder and contentment. She tried to turn her head and observe him fully, but he remained elusive and distant. Jenni could feel it was a male presence. She didn't know how but she just knew. Each waking, Jenni would try to recapture her dream; try to piece together the puzzle of his identity. As he continued to observe her, Jenni felt a sense of peace settle upon her. His presence somehow brought comfort to her pain and loneliness. She tried to engage him, tried to draw him into her dream more fully. She sensed a deep reluctance, a wave of regret that left her breathless. In the dawn, Jenni would awaken, her face wet with tears as she mourned for her own loss as well as a loss she could not explain.

With time, Jenni began to learn how to move freely within her dream. No longer was she an observer of her own actions but in control of them. Each night she would seek out new wonders, new glens and pools in which she would frolic. Each night, the same benevolent force regarded her conduct with silent appraisal.

One night, not long after she had been assigned to Chicago 3, Jenni's dreams changed. She drifted off to sleep as usual, eager to return to the land where she roamed free. Finding herself beside her favorite pool, Jenni shed her loose white shift and stepped naked into the crystal blue water. The edge of the pool was shelved, allowing her to stand waist high in the water. Beyond the rocky ledge the pool opened into a deep clear lagoon. The motion of her body in the still pool caused gentle ripples that lapped against her silky skin. Enjoying the sensation, Jenni threw back her head and laughed with unbounded joy. She paused as an unfamiliar sound reached her ears. It was a low rumble as if an animal growled in the dense trees beyond. Waiting to hear if anything was approaching, Jenni held her breath. When no further sound shattered the peaceful glade, she continued with her bathing. Dipping herself under the water then submerging, she repeated the pattern, finally emerging breathlessly at the surface. Flicking her long strawberry blond hair so it cascaded down the sun kissed flesh on her back, Jenni shivered. Chilled by the depth of the water, she decided to exit the pool and restore her body temperature. The large, smooth rocks that circled the pool provided a place to lay and feel the warmth of the sun on her bare flesh, and she eagerly climbed upon them, stretching out and basking in the glow of the fiery orb. As usual the perpetual presence lingered out of her reach, just at the edge of her vision, elusive yet constant.

The sun quickly did its work, and Jenni was soon aching for the feel of the cool water once again. She stood up, this time with the thought of diving from the rocks into depth of the pool. Smooth and slippery, the rocks proved to be a hazard for the adventurous diver as her foot slipped and she fell into the water, striking her head on the rock as she tumbled.

As water rushed into her body, quickly filling her lungs, Jenni sensed a blackness overwhelm her. Her eyes closed as she lost consciousness. Unsure if she were still dreaming, Jenni felt two strong hands pull her from the water across the hard surface of the rocks and onto the soft blanket of the grassy bank. Unable to open her eyes yet fully aware, she coughed as a deluge of water travelled through her body, anxious to make its escape. The same two hands turned her on her side as water spewed unceremoniously from her mouth. Gasping for air, Jenni forced her eyes open against the glare of the sun. Two dark eyes looked back at her from under a scowling set of eyebrows.

"What are you doing in my dream?" she said with her own frown matching his.

Pulling back from her and settling back on his knees, his eyes held hers.

"You fell," he answered, holding out her shift and turning his head as she pulled it hastily over her head.

"Thank you," she whispered, her throat still smarting from the submersion. Her hand briefly touched the tender lump that had formed on her forehead. She drew in her breath as pain pounded in her head.

Turning his head quickly, the man reached past Jenni and pulled a large looking leaf from a nearby plant.

"This might help," he said holding the large green triangle onto her wound.

Eye to eye, Jenni's gaze took in every detail of the man in front of her. His dark hair curled slightly over his ears and down onto the nape of his neck. His broad chest was bare and every inch of his muscled torso was golden brown. His waist tapered into narrow hips that were wrapped scantily in a cloth of purest white. She knew him. She felt as if she were looking at someone she had known for so long yet her eyes only just observed him. He was the figure in the shadows, the comforting presence in her dreams.

"It's you," she breathed as her hand reached out and inadvertently touched the solid wall of his chest.

"Hamen." He filled in his name then smiled wryly at her. "This has never happened before," he explained.

"How many dreams do you get into then?" Jenni asked, pulling her hand away stung by the thought hers may not be the only dreams he visited.

"Myself, only yours," he said quickly as if sensing her feeling of betrayal. He grabbed her hand and held it in his own. "My people often use the dreams of races to communicate. We rarely leave our world these days. The universe has become a place where we no longer feel safe."

"That I can understand," Jenni agreed. "There is much unrest among the races."

"Your people should never have entered space. You were not ready. The primitive urge to control has caused much damage."

Jenni flushed angrily and pulled her hand from his warm grasp. "What about the good we have done?" she argued. "Many races have come under our protection."

"Races that would not have needed protection before the greed of the human race polluted the universe."

"So, why save me?" Jenni's rage boiled up within her. "One less human to concern yourself with from the safety of your planet."

Hamen looked aghast. "I could not watch you drown. What do you think I am?"

"I am dreaming," Jenni said. "I would have woken up before I died."

"Not in this dream," Hamen said softly. "Don't you awaken each morn feeling as though you have lived each one of your dreams?"

"I do," Jenni acknowledged. "I swear my skin looks browner and my hair smells of the breeze." As she spoke she looked down at her arms that had indeed developed a darker tone in the light of the natural sunlight.

"You are in a place called Killanti. It is a place where dreams are a reality yet still remain a dream. The Trinz have selected you as one of The Elected. They have a purpose for you and I am your guide."

"A purpose for me? I don't understand," Jenni said.

"Some humans have a soul that is open to change. The Trinz aim to bring those souls together to build a new future across the universe.

"How can this be? I am in my bed. This is just a dream."

"It is, yet it is so much more," Hamen said mysteriously.

Jenni pulled herself up to her feet. "I have certainly been having some strange dreams lately," she mused. "So, if I was to do this," she continued recklessly, pulling Hamen to his feet and bringing her arms around his neck, "it would be real?" She leaned closer and touched her lips to his, pushing her tongue out to tease his closed mouth.

Hamen's arms came around Jenni's waist and he pulled her into his hard body. She could feel his desire pushing against her lower body, and her hips moved instinctively against him. The same low growl she thought she heard earlier came again from his parted lips as his tongue thrust into her pliant mouth.

A sensation beyond anything Jenni had ever felt before pulsed through her body. It started at her lips then blazed a trail through her body, pausing to stimulate her nipples and purged through to her inner core causing her knees to buckle.

"My people have lived millennia, and yet I have never experienced such sweetness," Hamen whispered low into Jenni's parted lips. His tongue tasted her then pulled back revealing a tongue that was divided in the middle and moved on both sides with reptilian grace. Each fork moved independently as he leaned back towards her, hungrily claiming another kiss.

Jenni's mouth was filed with the exploring tongue. It both filled and tasted, possessively claiming her. Jenni rubbed against him, terrified of what may lay hidden beneath the thin cloth between them. Whatever it was bulged against her as if struggling to be released.

Jenni had some experience with men. During her grueling training program, she often relaxed in the seedier bars of Lower Level 6. Here she would sit and watch the interactions of species as they attempted to bridge the cultural difference and find some comfort so very far from home. Often Jenni would return to her quarters alone, but on occasion she indulged in a little comfort of her own, usually fuelled by the intoxicating vapors of Garland (the steaming herb discovered in Foxtrot Zone that if mixed with liquid nitrogen and inhaled through a straw could simulate the effects of an old fashioned "skin full"). For a few credits it could be purchased at any bar and consumed with blissful release from the stresses of the day. Jenni had, so far, stuck to the human race, but she was not adverse to the potential of inter-species relationships. It was not as taboo as it had once been although many factions still favored pure blood races.

Jenni's mind was bombarded with the sensations of Hamen's kiss. His tongue was skilled at reaching erogenous zones inside her mouth she had never known existed. Jenni could not help but wonder what else that tongue of his could stimulate. As if reading her thoughts, Hamen chuckled, a low throaty laugh. He pulled back from the kiss, his dark eyes burning with desire.

"We should stop this," he said, his breath catching in his throat.

"Why?" Jenni's own eyes widening in surprise. This was, after all, her dream, and she was damn sure she did not want it to stop.

"It is not my mission to seduce you," he explained. "I am to lead you to a life more fulfilling; a place where you can live as you do here in your dreams."

"Such places no longer exist," Jenni spoke wistfully, "only in memory and legend."

"You are very wrong. Beyond the reach of your corrupt kind, planets have remained pure."

"I am sure I would not be dreaming such disrespect for my kind." Jenni felt her anger building once again. "I am sorry I even tried to kiss you now. This dream is turning into a nightmare!"

Hamen's expression darkened with rage of his own. "Do not speak of such things here," he warned. "The dark dreams belong in a different realm and," he added, stepping forward with a grim set to his mouth, "I believe you did more than try to kiss me. I think you were very successful. Perhaps I need to refresh your memory."

The vehement objection Jenni planned to make disappeared from her lips as Hamen's mouth moved quickly over hers. His tongue flicked over her lips with a delicate caress that made her lips part, inviting his more intimate exploration. Her sigh, was her consent as his assault began.

After the longest kiss Jenni ever experienced, she pulled away and threw back her head to gasp some fresh air. Hamen took full advantage of the graceful curve of her neck and ran a trail of burning kisses along her throat and down towards the rise of her ample breasts. Instinctively, her body arched towards him, thrusting the hardened peaks of her aroused nipples towards his hot, wet mouth. She cried out as his split tongue ventured to feast on the protruding nipples as they pressed through the fabric.

"No!" Hamen pulled away again, his eyes showing the depth of his confusion. "I am sorry. I should not have done that. I have observed you for so many dreams, and each time I yearned to speak with you, to touch you. I...you...in the water, you looked so inviting. It was torture to keep back."

"I still do not understand," Jenni tried to change the subject as her body still ached for his kisses, for his touch and what would inevitably follow.

"Your time is almost up for tonight," Hamen reminded her. "I will find you when you sleep tomorrow. It is all I can do. I will try to explain more and I think you will have more questions."

"And if I don't come? If I dream another dream?" Even as she spoke the words, Jenni knew it was a ridiculous notion. She dreamed the same dream for so long, she knew no other.

"You'll come." The certainty in his words matched what Jenni knew in her heart.

Chapter Two

Before the solemn looking panel, Hamen lowered his gaze. His feet suddenly seemed more interesting than the scrutiny of his elders.

"How did it transpire?" the middle figure asked for the third time, his frown expressing a mixture of confusion and disappointment.

"As I have said, father, she fell. Her head was struck and she submerged. I feared for her life."

Hamen reluctantly raised his head and met with the intense stare of his father. As well as his role of parent, Ju was on the Elder Panel responsible for the Killanti Project. It had taken Hamen several attempts to convince his father to allow him onto the Project; the risks to the mind of the participants were as yet unknown. Making telepathic connections across the expanse of the universe would inevitably take its toll on the minds of the Trinz that volunteered.

"It is unheard of for two to meet in such a place," Wren, the eldest of the three, stroked his long white beard as if the answer would be found in the rhythmic action.

"Did the two of you make physical contact?" Ju shuddered as he spoke the words.

"I pulled her from the pool," Hamen wisely stopped there; he knew adding the details of their tryst would have resulted in his banishment from the Killanti Project. If there was one thing Hamen was sure of, it was that he fully intended to return to Jenni that night and for many others besides. The sensation of her kiss and the feel of her eager body had kept him up during his own rest time and pacing the floor of his chamber.

The Trinz were an old race, some said as old as the universe itself. They had been through the primitive rites the humans were still enjoying, those of physically coupling and taking a mate. The Trinz had evolved a method of reproduction that took place in the clinical world of their highly advanced laboratories. Couples, without the demands of sexual intimacy, were more able to maintain steady, fulfilling relationships based on mutual respect and companionship. Without the tension of sexual jealousy or infidelity, separation was rare and contentment the norm. In Killanti, Hamen had been awakened to the ways of old and his body was a whirl of testosterone and lusty desire.

"It is imperative you return again today," Lori, the third member of the group counseled. She was blessed with a devout wisdom that afforded her authority in the panel. Her eyes sized up Hamen as she spoke. "We must discover more of this change in state. Discover if the wounds inflicted upon the human were transferred into her own wakening. Do you think you could initiate more physical contact with her?"

Hamen was sure Lori worded her question with a humorous lilt. His flush of color gave away his emotions yet his words remained admirably disinterested. "I could try," he drawled.

"Then that is settled," she smiled. "This is indeed an unprecedented development but we will monitor closely your reactions and responses."

A cloak of unease crept over Hamen. His liaison with Jenni would be discovered if his vital signs and reactions were monitored too closely while he was mind travelling to Killanti. He was sure as soon as he was with her again, his urge to hold and kiss her would prove too tempting to resist. His lower regions were already growing hard at the thought of her soft undivided tongue probing his mouth with gentle passion. The sensation that travelled through his body made him want to move and leave the stuffy room where three pairs of eyes regarded him with interest.

"May I take my leave?" Hamen asked.

Three heads nodded so he turned to leave.

"A word with you as you walk?" Wren called to him as he exited the room.

Coming alongside, the older man moved with surprising agility. They walked in silence for a while and Hamen sensed Wren was having difficulty forming his words.

"Not every Trinzian has left the old ways behind. I think you know which old ways I speak of," he finally admitted. "May I show you something?"

Puzzled, he followed Wren out of the main building and through several narrow laneways. At a door marked with a twisted emblem, Wren knocked loudly three times. A shutter opened and a man's face appeared.

"Oh, it's you!" he sneered. "Back already are you? And what have we here, a new recruit? The boss does not like strangers."

Hamen listened, puzzled by the exchange. He was even more puzzled by the response of the mild mannered leader of the Elder Panel who bit back in a ferocious tone.

"Tell your master that if I bring a young guest, it had better be to his liking or he may find himself looking for premises elsewhere."

At that, the door swung open and the pair were permitted entry into a dingy corridor which was adorned with pictures depicting scenes that fascinated Hamen. Males and females were cavorting in positions that brought the blood pumping back into the lower regions of Hamen's body. Furthermore, they made his mind turn to the soft curves of Jenni's body as she entered the pool.

"Like it, lad?" Wren's voice leered into Hamen's ear as he pushed him along the corridor. "Wait until you see the real thing!"

At the end of the hallway, a room opened up filled with bodies in various form of undress. Males and females were draped all over one another, and the sound of gasping and sighing filled the air. Men caressed the women who purred their pleasure as their eager eyes feasted on the young man who had stepped into their sexual den. Male parts were exposed and bulbous as they awaited the final release. Hamen choked on the heady smell of musky arousal. His body yearned to turn and flee back to the fresh aroma of the city outside. His eyes darted around the room, reluctant to linger too long on the intimate scenes that played out before him.

"This way," coaxed Wren. "Some of us prefer a little privacy."

An open door led them into a maze of corridors with rooms leading off in all directions. Numbers adorned the frames and names were displayed below. Ignoring the first few, Wren suddenly stopped. Door sixty-nine was slightly ajar with the name Trein written in bold script.

"You'll like this one," Wren said, his lips moist as he slavered his words, nodding his head up and down as he smiled and drooled. His hands propelled Hamen into the dimly lit room. "I'll be next door," he grinned like a simpleton.

As the door closed behind him, Hamen looked around the room. A girl reclined on a bed that took up most of the space. Beside her was a small table that held a casket and beyond that was another door leading to a wash house. The covers on the bed were a deep red, and the pillows sparkled with a golden hue. The girl herself was slight. Hamen judged her to be little more than a minor. Her shape was under developed and her skin was pale.

"What is your name?" he asked kindly.

"You can call me what you wish," she smiled with a glint in her eye.

"What do you parents call you?" Even to himself, Hamen sounded pompous.

"Slyvie," she replied. "Before they left me here, they called my Slyvie. Here I am known as Trein. Come on now, take off those garments and we can begin."

"Begin what?" Hamen was becoming increasingly frustrated by the place he had found himself in.

"Oh, you are one of those. I have heard of your sort from the other girls, but the ones who come in here to me have usually done this before. They like the young ones. Your sort usually goes for the more experienced girls. Shall I call someone else?"

"No, thank you, no," Hamen said quickly. He had a feeling that a "more experienced" girl may more than he could deal with. "What is my sort?"

"One who has never done it." She giggled, showing her age to be much younger than Hamen had first thought. "Before we became as we are now, we used to use our bodies to love each other. Now we have evolved, but many still seek that extra something so they come here, to us."

Hamen could not stop his body. The hardening he had been experiencing of late came upon him at once.

"That's it," Slyvie cooed, eyeing the bulging length evident under his small cloth covering. She stood up and came across the room towards him. "You use that and put it here." With one hand she cupped his straining erection and with the other she gestured to the valley between her legs, tantalizingly visible through her sheer garment.

Hamen gasped. The dark triangle of hair she gestured to made his throat dry and his manhood twitch. His balls ached with a desire unfamiliar to him. Then he smiled as thoughts of Jenni came into his head. Her own downy triangle of hair hid a secret place where he could bury himself. The though made him giddy with desire.

"I see you are getting the idea," Sylvie's voice broke into his thoughts. "Looks like you could be a fast learner."

"No!" Hamen started as he realized Slyvie's hand was still caressing his hard length and his body was responding to her touch. He stepped back and shook his head. "I cannot. There is another. I am sorry."

"Shame but I still want my credits," Slyvie retreated to the bed, shrugging her thin shoulders. "Forty." From within the casket, the girl pulled a credit transaction device and scanned the chip Hamen offered. "She will be a fortunate girl to receive your first love."

"I hope so," Hamen replied as he took his leave.

Rather than wait for Wren, Hamen made his way quickly through the seedy residence and into the brightness of the street. The duel suns of Trinz made the days bright and the absence of a moon made it pitch-black at night. No stars graced the inky night sky as they all shone too far away. Trinz was at the furthest reaches of the universe, and it sat nestled in its own small galaxy; a distant planet orbiting its twin suns.

Gasping in lungfuls of air, Hamen leaned on the warm grey wall of the building he had just evacuated. Never had he imagined such goings on, yet now that he had seen what pleasures the flesh could enjoy, he was burning with an inner fire only Jenni could sate. Images of her naked form, bent into the positions he had just observed, allowing him to taste and caress her the way he knew she would enjoy. Hamen shuddered. He could hardly wait to enter Killanti and see Jenni again.

Chapter Three

As Jenni took her seat in the flight room, her head pounded. The swelling was noticeable and the pulsing pain was almost more than she could bear. Una noticed it at once.

"Been working out in the holorooms again?" she teased good-naturedly.

It was well known among Jenni's colleagues that she often let off steam in battle simulations. The holorooms were designed for just such a purpose, a place where you could use credits to entertain yourself as you desired. Jenni's parents had been high up in the militia and always encouraged her in self-defense and battle training. As a result, Jenni was skilled in combat and enjoyed the challenge of simulated fight. Due to the recent advancement in technology, holorooms could now provide that extra edge of real injuries. Lately, Jenni had upped her level as she was determined to request a transfer to the militia training ship due to fly into the newly acquired Yankee Zone. She had no real ambition to join the armed forces, but the chance to navigate another unchartered zone thrilled her. As part of the crew of such vessels, basic military training was a distinct advantage.

Jenni smiled at the look of concern on her friend's face. Una had tried on several occasions to take Jenni "under her wing." This, so far, had only involved introducing Jenni to several single colleagues who Una deemed suitable for her young charge.

"I must have fallen out of bed," Jenni lied easily. "I woke up on the floor with my head feeling like I'd spent the night snorting Garland."

"Not much out there," Una said, laughing at Jenni's admission. Her eyebrows rose in a gesture of hopelessness. "This has got to be one of the worst Zones we've come across. Nothing much to conquer here."

"Una? Do you think we have polluted the universe?" Jenni chewed thoughtfully on her lip as she regarded her friend.

Una's head darted from side to side as if she expected guards to burst in and arrest them for treasonous talk. "You mustn't talk so," she scolded. "I have seen men disappear for less aboard ships such as this."

"But do you?" Jenni persisted.

"If we had not ventured beyond the Milky Way, we would have perished," Una retold the old story patiently. "We seek a world on which to settle; one where we may breathe free; a new Earth."

"I know all that," Jenni sighed, "but at what cost to the planets that do not suit us? We pillage their wealth and move on. When will it end?"

"What has started such talk?" Una looked around again. "Who have you been consorting with?"

Jenni held back from confiding in Una about her dream. Something felt wrong to her. Besides, she wasn't too sure she understood it herself yet, so how could she explain to another?

The rest of the shift passed uneventfully, and soon it was time to head back to her quarters. Jenni made a point of stopping at the holorooms. She knew sleep would elude her if she had not tired herself out before falling into bed. The session was well worth the ten credits she had handed over to the swarthy man who ran the thriving business. Jenni dreaded to think what other dalliances people paid for, especially since the reality filter had been introduced.

Moving home through the labyrinth of corridors, Jenni turned several times to check that she wasn't being followed. The downside of the holoroom was you often spent several minutes readjusting to the real world after a session. Facing battle made one's senses far more heightened, and any deviance from routine could trigger paranoia. Still, Jenni could not shake the feeling someone was watching her, and she was glad when the door to her rooms shut and locked securely behind her.

The food simulator was offering fresh pesto pasta which Jenni readily accepted. Contraband was available and she had cupboards full of items she had acquired through various sources but tonight the ease of the ship's offering was a welcome friend. The steaming meal was soon teleported into her room and she sat with her legs curled up on her large, soft recliner and enjoyed the flavors as they filled her mouth and satisfied her hunger.

Jenni had transported the chair along with a few other possessions from her home world. It was a reminder of the family she lost. Her mum would sit, much as she was now, and regale her with stories of time past, stories of Earth and its bountiful history. Jenni loved to hear of the oceans and continents, of animals and history, all confined now to the microchips of libraries and school rooms. In turn, Jenni's mum had listened to her own mother before her and so on, a strong line of women determined to install the rich heritage to each new generation.

Tonight though, Jenni's mind was fixed on another matter entirely. She was lost in thoughts of her semi-naked Adonis who had thrilled her with his kisses. She marveled again at the feel of his reptilian tongue as it darted in and out, exploring each corner of her pliant mouth. A trail of desire pooled with moisture in Jenni's core as she imagined the path that tongue may take tonight. Still bemused by the encounter, Jenni knew with a certainty that filled her body she would meet with Hamen again tonight, and their chemistry would lead to some further passion. The idea of it excited her, and she was soon restlessly pacing the floor, eager for sleep. A hot shower provided some respite for her pent up tension before she slipped between the cotton sheets and tried to free her mind to allow slumber to overtake her.

Several hours later, Jenni pulled herself up and swung her legs over the side of the bed. She growled in frustration as sleep eluded her. Time after time, she had closed her eyes and sought the sweet oblivion of dreaming. She longed to enter the world she now knew to be Killanti and seek out Hamen. She craved more knowledge of him and his people and how she could experience such a reality in her dreams without ever leaving her bed. Opening a small cupboard to the side of her bed, Jenni drew out a dusty glass bottle. The red and brown bird on the side and the words "The Famous Grouse" caused her to smile, remembering a happy memory. The drink had been a favorite tipple of her father, and he knew a man who could, for a substantial number of credits, procure him the odd bottle from time to time. Its age only served to mature the flavor and inflate the cost of such a luxury. The bottle that now sat in Jenni's grasp was one her father had not managed to finish before his untimely demise. Jenni herself was quite repulsed by the flavor, but she knew a large glass of it would help to empty her mind and aid her quest for sleep.

The amber liquid tumbled into the hastily rinsed toothbrush mug. Jenni lifted it to her lips, the scent already triggering her gag reflex. In great gulps, she downed the alcoholic beverage, totally wasting the vintage blend in her haste. Shuddering with revulsion, the last of the whiskey disappeared and Jenni banged the cup down on the bedside table. Almost at once, warmth spread through her body and caused her mind to blur slightly. The room seemed to spin as she lay focusing on the small white globes that lit her ceiling. Closing her eyes against the unwelcome sensation, Jenni felt herself drifting off into the blissful state of slumber. Her mouth curved into a slow smile as she anticipated the night ahead.

~ * ~

Hamen waited by the pool. His body was tight as he stood rigidly, betraying his emotion by the clasp of his fists and the grim set of his jaw.

Where was she? Why hadn't she come?

The slight movement in the trees beside him caused his head to jerk around. The sight of Jenni's approach sent a tingle through him. Her hair was damp and clung to her face before it cascaded around her shoulders in a golden haze. Her eyes sought him out, finding his and locking with them. It was like a jolt of electricity as their gaze held. Hamen frowned slightly as he saw a slight sway to Jenni's body. He sensed a difference in her but could not fathom it.

"I thought you wouldn't come." The rawness in Hamen's words conveyed a vulnerability he was afraid to show. He covered it quickly with a sharp, "You're late!"

"It is my dream, I will come when I please." Jenni closed the gap between them, her eyes blazing with outrage.

"You will come when I make it so," drawled Hamen as he encircled her waist with one fluid movement. His darkening eyes made it clear he intended to fulfil his devilish vow.

Jenni threw back her head and surrendered to his embrace, her submission fuelling the desire in Hamen. His tongue slid effortlessly into her parted lips. Her taste was unique today, a kind of malty flavor.

"Mmmmm," Jenni muttered. "Kiss me. I have missed you." Her arms gripped him and pulled him into the embrace.

Hamen groaned as Jenni's hips ground into him. He thrust his own body against her, circling his hips as he pushed into her. His length screamed out to bury itself inside her and find the place he now knew

22

would welcome him.

Pulling away, Jenni panted as she tried to regain her breath.

"How is this possible?" she demanded. "How can we be here together, like this? My head was sore today. The bump remained."

"I do not know," Hamen admitted, longing to pull her back into him but knowing she deserved some answers before she committed her body to him. He knew she would be his tonight, here in the paradise of Killanti. "I spoke with the elders of my race today. They too are totally mystified. I have been sent back to find out more. Even now, they are monitoring me as I interact with you."

"Monitoring you?" Jenni asked, her brow furrowed in confusion.

Hamen sensed that her mind was having difficulty concentrating. Her eyes seemed to be unfocussed and her movement labored.

"What ails you?" he asked, reaching for her hand as he spoke.

"I am feeling, well...drunk," she admitted, ending on a giggle.

"Drunk? You mean you have been consuming fermented beverages? Why?"

Jenni's face grew red and Hamen thought it was the prettiest thing he had ever seen.

"I could not sleep," she admitted shyly. "I took a drink of whiskey. It is a drink from Earth. My father had a taste for it. When he died, he left a bottle half empty. I have kept it."

As she spoke tears began to course down her cheeks. Hamen was horrified at her grief and, once again, pulled her into his embrace.

"Sssh now," he cooed, his hands caressing her as he offered words of comfort.

Again, Jenni's body responded to his touch. She lifted her head and offered her lips to his. Unable to restrain himself, Hamen bent down and crushed her mouth to his. His tongue darted into her mouth and pushed in, taking possession of her. This time a kiss was not enough. He needed to taste more of her, feel her skin with his mouth and find the source of her femininity.

With one quick movement, Hamen pulled off the white shift that covered Jenni. Beneath it, her naked skin glowed in the light of the bright sun. She urged him on with soft moans and pants of desire. Hamen breathed in the heady scent of the woman before him. Her skin was freshly washed and smelled of citrus. Hamen licked his lips and let the tips of his tongue begin a sensual assault on the skin before him.

Taking his time, Hamen kissed the woman before him. His own desire was building as he anticipated the pleasure to come. Jenni's own hands began a tentative search. Hamen encouraged her with low rumbles of appreciation, altering his tone when she touched the more sensitive areas.

Somehow, the pair had sunk to the lush grassy bed that lay below their feet. They now lay entwined in each other's arms, their bodies wrapped together as one as they touched.

~ * ~

Jenni purred as Hamen's skilful tongue traced a path of ecstasy over her exposed body. She had known they would come together tonight, but the speed of their coupling surprised her. She knew some of her inhibitions had been vanquished by the strength of the aged blend she downed before falling asleep, but the rest had been pure carnal desire and the chemistry that existed between them. Jenni bucked as wave after wave of desire beset her body.

Tentatively, her hand ran its own trail down Hamen's toned body. His guttural moans urged her on. She wondered what she would discover as her hand cupped the cloth wrap. Her hesitation caused Hamen to pause in his own exploration.

"I think you will find me anatomically the same as the human form," he smiled sexily, his eyes urging her to find out for herself.

"B...but your tongue," she stammered.

"You think me forked down there?" Hamen's amusement was evident as he studied her face.

"I did wonder," Jenni admitted, a deep red hue staining her cheeks.

"Merely an initiation." Hamen stuck out his tongue and wiggled the two halves independently. "It is done in families who respect the old ways. When a boy becomes of an age to be known as a man, he passes through certain rites. One is to have this done. It is just the way of things."

"Did it hurt?" Jenni reached out her hand and touched the split, fascinated by the independent movement.

Hamen shrugged. "I suppose it did," he said. "I can scarce remember. It is hurting that I am this close to you yet am not kissing or discovering more about your pleasure."

Jenni shivered as his obvious desire for her was spoken. She smiled up at him as he lowered his mouth to claim hers once again. This time his kisses moved quickly to her throat then ran to her breasts where he held each peachy orb and suckled the nipples with quiet murmurs of joy.

Jenni ran her hand up Hamen's thigh. The hairs tickled her palm as she moved higher up towards the place she longed to expose. Jenni gasped as a solid length met her touch. No under garments separated her from the firm flesh of his desire. Encouraged by Hamen's growl, Jenni ran her hand up and down, marveling at the size and girth of his sex. Fisting her hand around the erection, Jenni pumped up and down with increasing speed. Her thumb caressed a sphere of moisture that had pooled on the tip. She paused, eager to feel the size and width fill her and penetrate between her wet thighs.

"Please," she begged. "I'm ready."

"Oh, I am going to have to check that for myself," Hamen replied, bringing his head up from her breasts.

His hands found their way straight to her core. They parted through the downy hair and found the sensitive nub that lay nestled between the silky folds of skin. One hand lingered to toy with her there, whilst the other hand pushed deep into the place where she was wet and waiting. Hamen slid in two fingers then pulled them out before plunging them back in. His act simulated what she needed with every part of her body. The combination of sensation soon had Jenni cresting on a wave of orgasm. Her body pulsed around Hamen's fingers, and he continued his relentless course. Crying out, Jenni threw back her head and allowed the sensation to devour her.

Hamen withdrew from her and quickly replaced his hand with his own rigid member. Thrusting against her, he buried himself deeply inside before pulling back then entering her again. Over and over he thrust, keeping Jenni's orgasm ripping through her body. With one final stroke, Hamen barked her name then fell heavily against her. Their pounding hearts beating out the rhythm of their love making as, sated, they slowly regained their composure.

Hamen rolled off and Jenni snuggled into the solid wall of his body. He was warm yet the gentle breeze that blew cooled her skin and made her shiver.

"Are you cold?" he asked, his voice full of concern.

"A little," she said. "I am not used to a real breeze, but I rather like it."

Hamen reached for the sarong that lay beside them and draped it over her body.

"Your arms are warmer." Jenni burrowed in closer to his radiating heat. "I wonder what the monitors will make of what just happened?" she giggled.

Hamen's chest rumbled as he joined in with her mirth. "I may be in trouble when I return," he agreed.

"If our physical bodies are not here, how did we manage that?" Jenni asked.

"That I am unable to answer," Hamen admitted. "When we find a human we choose to recruit, the process is usually to guide their dreams and speak into their minds. With you I have been unable to approach. I have watched you explore and enjoy Killanti but without the ability to communicate."

"I knew you were there but I could not engage you or see you. I just sensed you somehow. When you pulled me from the pool, it was as if I knew you," Jenni frowned as she tried to make sense of the situation.

"Yes." Hamen absentmindedly stroked her back as he replied, "We have had a connection but nothing like any other. It is a mystery to me and to the Elder Panel who monitor all the Communers."

"Communers?" Jenni's eyebrows arched with the question.

"It is what we call ourselves. The group of us that commune with the humans. We have successfully populated several worlds over the years; worlds that live in peace and harmony with nature and the resources they possess."

"I have never heard of such worlds," Jenni remarked. "Where are they?"

"Their location is kept a secret until the humans commit themselves and seek out a new life. Through dreams we can act as guides across the universe."

"And you wanted me for one of these worlds?" Jenni asked.

"Yes. You have an aura of hope and joy. We found your light among much darkness."

"How? How did you find me?" Jenni was confused.

27

Hamen's hand had begun to stroke her back with a persistence that was firing up her desire once again. Heat pooled between her legs and her breath grew short.

"Dreams," he cooed, "take us out of ourselves. Our minds are freed and the footprint of such a journey makes its mark upon the universe. My people have technology that picks up such activity, analyzes it and feels the hopes and despairs of races. It is how we first sought out humankind, heard their pleas for help; their prayers, if you will."

"So, when we seek a higher being, a god, some order to the chaos, that is you?" Jenni recalled the silent prayers she had offered to save her parents and bring them home to her.

"We have no power to alter destiny," Hamen's voice was laced with regret. "We hear the pain but cannot come to the aid of every heartache."

Tears had begun to roll down Jenni's cheeks. Suddenly, every dream and wish she had seemed defiled somehow like she was just a microscopical part of some greater experiment, being watched and judged by a superior race.

"Why do your people trouble themselves about such inferior races?" Jenni's temper was riled again. "Are we just playthings for your amusement?"

Hamen gripped Jenni's face and looked deeply into her eyes. "Your race fascinates us," he explained. "You are full of such complex emotions. You have such capacity to love and grow, yet you destroy and hate. We strive to guide you to a place where you can reach the potential we see in you. Our goal is to give you a future."

His lips fell upon hers and his kisses were urgent. Jenni stirred under his passion, unable to resist its raw hunger. She returned the kiss, moving her hands to bury themselves in the thickness of his hair.

"Jenni," he spoke against her lips. "I want to taste you."

Jenni gasped as he pulled away and smiled slowly. She watched mesmerized as he lowered his head and gently parted her legs, exposing the soft tender flesh of her womanhood. Maintaining eye contact, Hamen lowered his head slowly and finally disappeared between the valley of her legs. Jenni realized that she held her breath. Her lip was between her teeth as she waited for what would transpire. Images of the flicking tongue delighted her mouth, filled her mind.

A light touch made Jenni's hips buck. It was followed by another then another. Hamen's hands cupped Jenni's rear and held her fast. His tongue moved quickly yet so lightly over her swollen nub. Each lick was filled with the promise of so much more and Jenni moaned in delightful frustration.

~ * ~

Hamen circled his tongue around and over the sensitive button that was the key to Jenni's desire. Her bucking was driving him crazy, and he yearned to bury himself into her hot, wet body once again. The way she had clenched against him was a sensation he wanted to experience over and over. Suddenly, he could see why some of his people still craved this contact, this intimacy. He wondered why they had evolved from such sinful delights. Using his tongue, Hamen could push inside her whilst still stimulating her rim. He upped his pressure and teased relentlessly until he felt Jenni shudder and clasp against him. Licking and tasting her pleasure, Hamen savored the musky flavor of her arousal. Unable to control his own needs a moment longer, Hamen rose over her and guided himself into the welcoming warmth that opened for him. Loving the way he filled her, he drove in hard, circling his hips to burrow deep inside. Too soon, he was cresting on the verge of release. His body tensed as his seed erupted within her. Her own cries mixed with his as together they came on a wave of utter submission.

Spent, they rested, skin to skin on the damp grass. Hamen knew their time was almost at an end. Her night and his day were each ending. He dreaded what awaited him upon his return.

Will they allow me to return to her after this or would she now be deemed unsuitable for relocation?

Deep down, Hamen knew. He knew their actions would have jeopardized her place in paradise. Therefore, she would be of no more use to the Project despite their unique connection. That in itself endangered the mission and made the Trinz vulnerable. No, he was sure after tonight he would not be permitted to return to Killanti with Jenni. She would no longer be considered suitable as one of The Elected. A sharp pain ran through his body as the force of his grief hit him. A tearing sound ripped through the air and he sat up clutching at his chest in agony.

"What is it?" Jenni sat up, laying her hands on his chest, her eyes wide in alarm.

"I...I...do not know. It feels like I am being ripped apart." Spasms racked Hamen's body as the pain intensified. "I...love you," he gasped as he fell back, unconscious on the ground.

~ * ~

Jenni looked around. There was nothing she could do, no one to help. It was her dream and any minute now she would awaken. Her thoughts raced through her head.

What if something had happened to Hamen's body? What if he had been pulled from the machines that maintained him?

She knew their bodies remained in their own reality, yet somehow the power of their minds made their bodies physical in Killanti. Jenni

30

likened it to the Holorooms where reality was suspended and another reality imposed upon your mind. That was common practice in her world, so she assumed beings more evolved than her own race could have more advanced and superior technology.

Jenni was at a loss. She knew she was powerless in this place, but she vowed to seek out the Trinz and find out what had befallen Hamen. One night with him had convinced her that she would like to repeat the experience, and the idea of living in a world like the one she had visited in her dreams was very attractive to her indeed. Feeling her eyes close, the signal that her dream was ending, Jenni curled up and clung to the body that had, just moments ago, taken her to places she had never seen before.

"I will find you!" she vowed as she too slipped from the realm of Killanti.

Chapter Four

Wake up call for Jenni Gravin! Wake up call for Jenni Gravin!
The computer generated alarm persisted, requiring voice activation to silence it. Jenni groaned as she turned over and stretched her body. Her arms flung out to the sides, the right one coming into contact with a firm, warm obstacle. Jenni's eyes opened in horror as she realized someone was in her bed. The droning alarm continued as Jenni froze, afraid to look to the body beside her. She looked at the empty cup beside her bed and remembered the whiskey. Surely she hadn't been out and brought someone back with her.

"What is that noise?" a familiar voice moaned. "Someone stop it."

"Hamen?" Jenni whispered, finally turning her head to see the figure beside her.

"Jenni?" he replied, his voice echoing her confusion. "Where are we and what is that infernal racket?"

"Alarm stop!" Jenni called, instantly silencing the robotic voice. "Hamen, you are in my bed."

"Hmmm," Hamen said his voice low in his throat. "Enough information for now."

His hands pulled her on top of him and reached up to slide themselves under her shift. "Did I not dispense with this thing last time?"

"Hamen!" Jenni struggled to resist the pounding need that had risen within her as she tried to free herself from Hamen's vice like grip. "You are in my bed! My bed. In my room. On my spaceship!"

"So soft," Hamen murmured, caressing her skin and cupping her breasts in his hands, His thumbs moved gently across her nipples, and he sighed with deep contentment as he teased them to rigid peaks.

Jenni squirmed against his touch, rotating her hips against his masculine hardness. She was rapidly losing her train of thoughts as the lustful desires of her treacherous body overwhelmed common sense. Sighing, she threw back her head and moaned.

Hamen paused to lift her onto his rigid shaft, and she purred as he took control of lowering her slowly to take the whole of him. When his hands returned to her breasts, she began to take the lead. Her hips ground down onto him as she savored the sensation of his length inside her. Her orgasm was already building as the course sensation of his pubic hair rubbed against her sensitive clitoris. The delicious friction combined with Hamen's sensual assault of her nipples soon had Jenni panting for release. When it came, she was joined by the shouts of Hamen as he too found the heady heights of delight.

Several moments passed before Hamen's ragged voice broke the silence.

"I am in your bed," he observed. "In your room. On your spaceship."

"I know," Jenni replied. "It is what I was trying to say before I was so beautifully interrupted."

"But why? What has happened? How can I be here?" Hamen's confusion was evident.

"Your guess is as good as mine," Jenni shrugged. "I woke up and there you were."

Hamen stood up and paced around the bed. His eyebrows were

drawn in a frown as he mumbled to himself.

"I am sorry if here is not where you would like to be," Jenni's hurt tone betrayed the emotion she was feeling.

Hamen stopped and looked down at her. "Here is the very place I want to be," he said sincerely. "I am just puzzled as to why and how it is possible. I was convinced I would not be permitted to see you again after...well after what happened between us."

Jenni looked down shyly. "Maybe they had no control over it," she mused. "Maybe the universe intervened to bring us together."

Jenni rose from the bed and pulled on her uniform. The light slacks and tunic were in deep crimson and set off her golden skin to perfection.

"Where are you going?" Hamen asked.

"I have to work," she explained. "I think I must keep some semblance of order. If you were discovered aboard with no papers, you would be arrested and transported to one of the prison worlds."

"You have whole worlds that are prisons?" Hamen voiced his disgust. "Your kind never ceases to repulse me."

"What do you do with wrong doers then?" Jenni snapped, unable to prevent herself jumping to the aid of her kind at his attacks.

"We run highly successful rehabilitations programs," he explained.

"Aka mind wipes, I suppose," Jenni bit out her smarting retort.

"There is a level of mind control, yes." Hamen seemed un-phased by the ways of his kind.

"We prefer freewill here," Jenni smiled in triumph. "Now stay here and I will be back as soon as I can. If you want to eat, there is food in the kitchen."

Jenni was reluctant to leave him behind, but she was already running late and would have to take the overcrowded shuttle rather than walk as she normally would. When she arrived, she was flushed and agitated. Her mind was focused on Hamen and her daily tasks seemed cumbersome. Una urged her to return to her quarters. She voiced her concern as the younger girl failed to notice a band of asteroids, and the ship had to maneuver evasively to avoid them. Jenni managed to see out her shift but was relieved when the computer signaled the hand over time had begun. Declining an offer of a coffee and chat, Jenni jumped on board the shuttle, hoping it would return her more promptly to Hamen.

What if he's vanished? What if it had just been an extension of my dream?

Her head was filled with worries until she stood and saw the familiar broad shoulders hunched over her computer table.

The screen was alive with images and maps. Stars, flashed by as planets came and went. Hamen's hands moved with lightning speed as he pulled in pages and information to the web of knowledge.

"Someone's been busy," she said softly, her eyes never leaving him.

As Hamen turned around, Jenni's heart lurched with pleasure as she witnessed the look of joy that crossed Hamen's face.

"It took some digging and access to some sites I probably shouldn't have been able to enter, but I think I have a few answers," his eyes lingered on Jenni's lips as he spoke.

Responding to his scrutiny, Jenni's tongue poked out and licked her lips. His gaze had made them dry, and her tongue rasped along, tracing their shape to hydrate them.

"I thought the shift would never end," Jenni admitted. "Then I thought you may have just been a figment of my imagination."

"Shall I show you how real I am?" Hamen's challenge hung between them as he stood up and opened his arms in an invitation.

Jenni moved towards him as if pulled by an invisible string. She was soon standing against his chest, her arms feeling the planes of his muscled back. She lifted her head to accept his kiss then allowed herself to bask in the heady sensations his skilled tongue could evoke.

Groaning with the pain of separation yet feeling the grumbling protests of her empty stomach, Jenni broke the contact and smiled an apology.

"My body craves more than just love," she explained as a low rumble of agreement came from within her.

Embarrassed, she shrugged and giggled. "Food. I need food."

Hamen nodded reluctantly. "I too could use some sustenance," he agreed. "What is on offer?"

Jenni tried to ignore the cheeky smile that accompanied his words. This man was a distraction she could see herself getting quite used to.

"The food simulator is offering sticky ribs with mashed vegetables, or I have a cupboard full of acquired delights," she said, reading off the screen beside the food replicating machine.

"What delights could you provide?" Hamen asked with a wolfish grin.

"For now, an omelette with cheese and salad," Jenni tried to ignore the dark, brooding eyes that invited so much more. "Make yourself useful and crack these," she said passing him a carton of eggs from the chiller.

"Crack?" he asked with bewildered awe.

Jenni raised her eyebrows with mock severity then skillfully demonstrated the process. "Don't get any shell in it," she warned.

Hamen seemed to enjoy the task, although much of the congealed albumen adored the smooth work surface when he was complete. Jenni took the bowl and added seasoning and a dash of milk before beating the mixture lightly with a fork. She pulled a flat griddle pan from a hook above her head and pressed an icon on the smooth glass control panel that lay beside a digital hot plate.

"It is an indulgence to have one of these," she admitted,

"Particularly since the power shortages but I do prefer the taste of a home cooked meal. It comes from growing up on a planet, I suppose."

"We heat nothing," Hamen watched in obvious fascination as Jenni pottered about. "Everything is fresh and gathered from each garden or growing farm. Our milk is processed from nuts. No animal products have ever been used by the Trinz, but I have read about the way humans eat much from other living things."

"Something else for you to disapprove of, I suppose," snapped Jenni.

Hamen shrugged. "A fact, that is all. Your species is less evolved than us. Our bodies have no use for the nutrients that yours require."

"Hmm," Jenni mused as she poured the mixture onto the steaming hot-plate.

The smell filled her nostrils at once and made her mouth salivate. She added cheese and flipped the disk shaped omelette over to create a golden semi-circle. A few more minutes solidified the egg and melted the cheese before Jenni slid it onto the waiting plate. Decorating the plate with a handful of pre-made salad, Jenni pushed it towards Hamen and set about creating a replica for herself. Jenni watched out of the corner of her eyes as Hamen tucked into the salad and pushed the omelette suspiciously around his plate.

"I'll have you know my omelettes are the talk of the vessel," she teased.

"Oh yes, and how many other males come here to your quarters and feast with you?" Hamen's voiced growled in his chest.

He walked up behind her and reached around her waist, pulling her roughly against his hardness.

"There will never be another," he vowed as he ground his hips against her.

Jenni felt her core come alive. She ached to have him in her and to dominate her. Bending forwards over the shiny worktop, she reached to her trousers and pulled them down, revealing the lacy covering that lay beneath.

~ * ~

Hamen took over. He pulled the material to one side and removed his own garments. Wasting no time, he thrust deep inside her, not stopping until his body smashed against her, telling him that she had his full length inside her. The thoughts brought him close to climax and he paused, taming his mind to prolong the pleasure. Jenni mewed as he stopped, rotating her hips to spur him on. Longing and desire merged in Hamen's head as he withdrew and entered her again and again. He could smell her musky arousal and it was driving him wild. Again and again, he met her skin and sank deep inside her. He looked down at her bent form and saw his length entering her and disappearing from sight. The soft folds of her womanhood parted for him and he roared his desire.

Jenni reached back and grabbed his hand. Her breath was coming in pants of pure arousal. Hamen knew she was as close to fulfilment as he was, and he was glad to know they would come together. Jenni guided his hand to her buttocks and extended his finger, lining it up with her anus. Hamen almost exploded as he slipped his finger into her and heard her scream his name. Her body milked his as his salty seed burst from him. Adding his cries to hers, the pair reached a mutual crescendo of raw, uninhibited passion.

"That is why you will never be with another," Hamen boasted as he helped Jenni to stand and offered her the plate of food she had discarded.

Hamen watched in awe as she righted her clothing and moved to the soft comfort of the lounge area. She tucked her legs under her like a girl and ate hungrily. Soon the plate was empty, and Jenni looked up at him with a slow smile.

"My two favourite things done; how was your day?"

Hamen laughed. His heart felt light and full of joy. This amazing woman in front of him was coolly accepting of the bizarre chain of events that had led him to her.

"So, what did you discover?" Jenni asked.

"It seems the Killanti Project was run once before. It is in its second wave of operation. Something went wrong with the first wave, and it was abandoned. The Elder Panel included Wren, my father and one other. The third man took the blame for the whole fiasco and was banished from Trinz. I have located him on a planet in what is now termed as The Quebec Zone. I plan to secure a vessel and go there to meet him. He may have some answers."

"Don't you want to go home?" Jenni asked in a small voice.

Hamen felt a wave of protective instinct fill him. "I have found you now. I will not go back unless you are with me. Alone, I would never be able to see you again."

Hamen was rewarded with a grateful look, filled with feeling. He silently cursed his people for breeding all such thoughts and emotions from their DNA.

"I believe we can release one of the smaller, run around craft. It can hold enough fuel to get us to the closest refueling station."

"You really have done your homework," Jenni praised. "How do you propose to get through security and how will we cover my absence."

"I have set up a fictitious recognizance mission and your name is on the order. I found a General Lio who seemed to have enough authority to be feasible. It is all set up for tomorrow."

"General Lio," Jenni's face fell. "He is the man who led my parents to their death. He is responsible for many of the atrocities you blame my race for. He is the force behind the deep space exploration. It is as if he seeks something he has not yet found. The man is relentless. I hope he never finds out about your deception in his name."

~ * ~

Even the name sent shivers up Jenni's spine. Her mind raced with pictures of death and destruction. Jenni had never laid eyes on General Lio herself, but she knew of his fearsome reputation. Her parents had served him well, but since their deaths, his power had grown and his ambition knew no bounds. Head of deep space exploration, his will drove the human race deeper and deeper into the universe, never sated, always hungry to devour more worlds and discover new races. His ultimate goal was to reach the end of the universe, a duel star system yet unchartered and unmapped. Jenni offered a prayer to whoever was up there that the General would not hear of what had been done in his name to secure the vessel.

"Maybe we had better get some sleep," Jenni suggested. "I don't think I will be dreaming tonight."

"No need to dream of me," Hamen said. "I will be right here."

Jenni stripped off her uniform and slipped into the comfort of her night shift. She pulled back the covers on the neatly made bed and wriggled to find the familiar dent.

"What if you are not here when I wake?" Jenni asked as Hamen joined her under the covers.

"Hold my hand," he reassured her. "Then I cannot slip away."

Jenni decided she would go one better than that. She snuggled against his chest, finding the warmth of his skin a comfort.

Please be here when I waken, she willed as sleep overtook her.

Chapter Five

Cal looked across his white, crystal topped desk and regarded the man who faced him. Anxiety was etched on the brow of the older man, and he fiddled with his white beard in obvious distress.

"What do you mean he disappeared?" Cal snapped, quickly running out of patience with the bumbling leader of the Elder Panel.

"I mean just as I say," Wren answered. "One minute he was there and the next he sort of faded from sight. One of the mind technicians approached the pod just as his form vanished."

"What is to be my gain in assisting the Elder Panel?" Cal asked.

Wren's face reddened with evident anger. "You exist here because of an unfortunate incident, yet you have chosen to infiltrate and corrupt our utopian society."

"Nothing can be corrupted that does not wish to be," Cal smiled as he recalled the desperation of the Trinz to return to their primal roots. His human experience and eye for potential profit made his venture a sweet success. There was never any shortage of takers for his girls, or his boys, come to that.

"Maybe," Wren agreed. "I must admit to being rather partial to a particular young lady in your employ."

On Earth, Cal had always been an upright citizen. His time had been spent advising his superiors on the environmental suitability of planets. He had been born of two human parents and aspired, as did many of his species, to find a world that best represented the home world of Earth. With his qualifications in atmospheric biology, he was in a better position than most to assess the potential for each newly discovered planet.

It was whilst on the ecologically and atmospherically bountiful planet of Aphrodite North in the Lima Zone when Cal's dreams started. He would crave sleep, longing to return to the paradise his dreams created night after night. The lush green of the grass, the pure freshness of the water and the ripe sweetness of the fruits that grew there thrilled his very soul and made his senses soar. Days were spent yearning for the night which when they came, were filled with sensual delights. But then one particular night, he saw her. She was sitting among the verdant grass, picking flowers and gathering them into a full bouquet. She was the most beautiful girl Cal had ever seen. Her waves of chestnut colored hair fell in perfect ringlets down the smooth contours of her back; her toned, naked young body moved freely and uninhibited in the meadow. Cal stood mesmerized by the vision he beheld. It was his dream, yet somehow knew she had not been conjured by his imagination.

When she turned, alerted somehow by his presence, her face reflected the shock and fascination of his own. Night after night they had met, come together and loved; loved as he had never loved before. She confessed her mission was to bring him to a place she called Killanti. She explained how she had travelled through his dreams across the universe to find him and guide him to the Eden her people had created. Cal would have followed her anywhere.

One night she came to him with a new desperation. They mated with their usual passion, but he sensed in her a frenzy that both thrilled and troubled him. Breaking down in tears, she confessed she had been betrothed to another and would be pulled from the Project. Cal grieved with her as he sought a way to prevent himself from waking. His heart was breaking as they bid a final farewell.

When Cal awoke, he had found himself in a sterile cell. He was left there for many days until a man with a long brown beard came to discuss his future. It soon became obvious Cal had been transported across the universe in some strange anomaly. He begged to be reunited with his love but found himself a prisoner in a luxury underground home. Too scared to send him home, the Trinz feared the exposure his return may bring. Unable to reside in Trinz society for fear he would cause too many questions for the new and high priority Killanti Project, Cal remained, for all intents and purposes, incarcerated.

His love turned to despair then to fury, finally settling on revenge. Cal worked to manipulate Wren, the man who served as his protector and jailer. As his only companion, Cal discovered the celibacy of the Trinz. He still felt the flames of the passion he had shared with one of these supposedly passionless people and began to plot his vengeance. Cal spoke to Wren of desire and passion. He painted a visual picture of the pleasure and fantasies that could be shared between two willing souls. Soon Wren was begging for a chance to experience it for himself. Cal laid out the things he would need and waited until Wren delivered the goods. One night he arrived with a buxom young woman and disappeared into the prepared boudoir to experience his first taste of the sins of the flesh. Insatiable for more, Wren was soon visiting as often as he could. He began arriving with additional men who were fascinated by the sordid den. A man of influence could make things happen in any society and, before long, Cal was running a profitable brothel. Credits poured in but the satisfaction for Cal was that he was responsible for the corruption of the cold hearted race who had broken his heart.

"None have passed through since you," Wren broke into Cal's

reminiscing. "What made it so?"

"Love. Desperation. Who knows?" Cal retorted. "I have never been privy to the identity of the woman who brought me here. Maybe she would know. Did any others know of my arrival?"

Wren paused. "There was one other," he said. "He made up the third member of the Elder Panel. He has since left Trinz. Maybe he has the answers."

"Then I suggest you find him and leave me out of it!" Cal snapped.

He sank back into his chair, an image of chestnut hair flashed into his mind and a tear appeared at the corner of his eye.

~ * ~

Across town the eyes of another were filled with tears; tears for a lost son. Rein looked across at her husband, Ju.

"Why didn't you tell me?" she sobbed.

"I knew it would upset you," he said, trying to reason with his distraught wife. "I know you still think of him. I thought it would bring it all back."

Rein looked away, ashamed. She did think of Cal, often. She was happy in her marriage and the birth of Hamen had been the distraction they both needed to move on from her shame. Her quarantine for nine months after the "incident" had been attributed to stress. Mind travel often caused stress to the brain, and participants regularly needed leaves of absence to regain their mental strength. The fact the couple had been blessed by a child when they returned to the city had not been in the least unusual.

Ju had been a tower of strength at the birth and had found a discreet nurse who had traveled space and had experience in the rudimentary process of natural birth. If she thought it unusual the young couple had not favored the conventional method of artificial insemination in a surrogate mother who would be kept in a secure medical facility for the duration of her pregnancy, she kept it to herself.

"I told you not to use him," Rein attacked her placid husband. "He must have it in his DNA to move through space."

"Nonsense," Ju spoke softly. "He was tested and came up as a most suitable candidate. It is a macabre coincidence, nothing more."

Rein looked back at her husband. She knew he did not believe that any more than she did.

"Where is he?" Rein asked.

"We have calculated it to be somewhere in the Romeo Zone," he informed her.

The irony was not lost of Rein. She had studied Earth literature and had mooned over the romantic love Shakespeare encapsulated in his work.

"Will he be brought home?" she asked.

Ju nodded. "We need to find the cause of this malfunction. We are too close to success to let one mishap ruin our plans."

"Mishap! Malfunction! That is my son you are talking about. He could be in all manner of danger."

"Your son, yes," Ju said sadly.

"What if they meet?" Rein was too upset to notice the slump of her husband's shoulders at her impulsive words. "What if Hamen meets his father?"

Again, Rein failed to notice the change in the behavior of her husband. His averted eyes and guilty flush were lost on the grieving woman.

"We'll find him and bring him home," he assured her.

Chapter Six

Jenni's body was filled with a rush of adrenalin as she crept through the ventilation system. Her heart was thumping so loudly she was surprised the whole seeker ship could not hear her. On her hands and knees behind Hamen, Jenni reflected on the last twenty-four hours of her life. Her gaze travelled over the swaying buttocks of the man who was her guide through the maze of metal tunnels that would lead them to the hanger where the small run-around vessel awaited them. Hamen had fabricated an order for an exploration to a nearby planet. He insinuated that General Lio had intelligence the planet may contain much needed supplies for the militia ships. Jenni was his cover as her navigational expertise was renowned on Chicago 3, or anywhere else she had worked for that matter.

Up ahead, Hamen had stopped. Jenni, lost on her own thoughts, had been oblivious and careened into his behind with a hefty smack.

"Now, now," Hamen teased, "you will have to restrain yourself until we get aboard."

Jenni felt the familiar sensation of a flush creeping into her cheeks. "I was just distracted," she admitted.

"Remember the plan," Hamen's tone lost its joviality and turned serious. "You will need to drop down here and go through security. I will crawl on until I get to the other side of the door. You can then unlock the vent and we'll board. I may have been able to fabricate an order from the General, but I did not have time to create a security clearance for myself. I will work on that whilst we are aboard. It will make things easier when we arrive on any planet or ship. I don't want to spend my whole life crawling through ventilation shafts."

"The view is quite good from my end!" It was Jenni's turn to tease.

"I'll have to remember that and let you go first next time," Hamen retorted.

Jenni's body tingled at the timbre of his words.

"Tell me again why I had to crawl this far in the tunnels with you instead of getting there on foot? I am not the stowaway." Jenni struggled to adjust her body to a position that allowed her to drop through the hole.

"It avoided any awkward conversations," Hamen replied, "and kept me company."

Jenni laughed as he helped lower her down to the ground.

"Say as little as possible and get through quickly," Hamen coached her.

Jenni gave him a quick thumbs up then watched as he reapplied the louvered vent entrance. As he disappeared from view, she proceeded to the closed door labelled, "Hanger." Using her retina to open the door, Jenni came face to face with one of her old co-workers.

"Jenni," he greeted. "Long time no see."

"Hi, Yosi," she replied. "How is the security business treating you?"

"Can't complain. It is not quite as interesting as being on the top deck but the credits are good. Now, I need to scan you before take-off. Selected personally by Lio, I hear." His voice held a tone of awe.

"My parents served him," she explained as briefly as she could.

Yosi had made no secret of his attraction to her, and it seemed his interest had not diminished. His eyes roved over her in a most intrusive way, lingering over her curves.

"A shame we have done away with strip searches," he leered.

A sudden crash from overhead caused the pair to jump, startled by the racket.

"What the fuck was that?" Yosi spluttered. "Felt like the whole roof was coming down on us."

"Malfunction in the cooling system, perhaps," Jenni said calmly. "You had better report it when you have finished with me."

"Oh, I haven't even started with you," he quipped in a low tone. "How about we get together over a snifter of Garland when you return?"

"Mmmm! Sounds great." Jenni played along to ensure the smooth running of her departure.

A growl echoed through the overhead pipes, causing Yosi to glance nervously upwards.

"Let's move on," Jenni suggested brightly. "If this roof is unstable, I would rather be standing somewhere else."

Yosi nodded and led her into a smaller room where a short tunnel filled most of the space. It was connected to a large screen with a stool in front of it.

"You know the drill," Yosi indicated to the entrance of the machine.

Jenni walked through slowly, allowing the scanner to pass over her body. It tingled slightly but caused no pain. At the other end, Yosi nodded his approval.

"All clear," he advised. "Yours is in Bay 29."

"Thank you, Yosi. I look forward to seeing you on my return," Jenni lied smoothly.

"I will be looking out for you," Yosi promised.

Jenni moved out of the scanning room and quickly across the vast expanse of the hanger floor. Run around ships of various sizes filled the space, each in numbered bays. Hamen had thought of everything and secured a vessel that sat in the furthest bay from the control room. As she approached, she heard a gentle metallic tapping coming from the large ventilation shaft on a nearby wall.

"Who is it?" Jenni joked as she angled the grill up and out, removing it in one fluid motion.

Hamen emerged, shooting her a furious stare.

"Finished with your boyfriend?" he demanded.

"I was just being nice. I did not want to alert him to my eagerness to leave," Jenni explained.

Hamen harrumphed and dragged her the short distance to the small vessel. The boarding door stood open, and they climbed in making straight for the pilot seats. Jenni tucked her bag in an overhead compartment before she settled in the large, soft seat and pushed a green button that shut the doors behind them.

"Last step," Hamen said. "Get us out of here."

Jenni nodded then fixed an earpiece to her right ear, pulling the microphone down in line with her jaw.

"Request from bay twenty-nine to open hanger doors," she said clearly.

"Start your engine," came the reply.

Jenni waved her hand over the sensor and heard the purr of the engine. She pressed her fingers against the interactive screen and guided the vessel to hover above the ground. The side of the space craft opened to reveal a galaxy of stars. Jenni steered her small ship skillfully towards the inky blackness.

"Attention, vessel twenty-nine," a voice boomed in her ear. "Life sign scan reports two bodies within the ship. Please advise. You are not clear for takeoff. Repeat, you are not clear for takeoff!"

"Fly!" Hamen barked.

Jenni increased the speed and headed for the opening. She gasped in alarm as the door began to close.

"Faster!" Hamen's voice was firm but calm. "Focus on what is open."

Obeying his command, Jenni looked at the decreasing gap before her. She used her hands to guide the ship, turning it slightly onto its side to make clearance.

"Phew!" she breathed as the doors snapped closed behind them.

"We have a slight head start," Hamen calculated. "We will proceed to the closest planet and change ships."

"That will be Columbia 2," Jenni brought up a visual of the purple sphere and changed their course. "There is a private docking bay in the northern hemisphere. It will be less populated and we should find a willing trader. Government ships are coveted due to their advanced technology. We will be tracked though."

"Leave that to me," Hamen said. "I can alter our flight path and delete any trace of our fuel footprint."

"Wow!" Jenni was impressed. "You can make us disappear?"

"Smoke and mirrors," Hamen admitted. "I will just program a false trail. It will buy us some time."

The next few hours were spent in a companionable silence as the pair worked side by side to complete their set tasks. Every so often they would lock eyes and a promise of passion would smolder between them.

Hamen read the screen as the planet grew closer. "The private docking area on a small island in the northern hemisphere of Columbia 2 is owned by a retired Sringey general. His name is General T. Goaf. The Sringey have been humankind's biggest opposition since the early days of the colonization, but since the Treaty of Unification, the two species live in relative peace, each benefitting from what the other can offer. As well as being strong in battle, the Sringey are a wealthy race and bask in the increased trade opportunities across the universe. They are found on most planets and space stations, usually turning a profit and always living in enviable luxury.

"General T. Goaf is no exception to this. He has made his money defending his people and has been rewarded handsomely for his efforts. He now lives on his own private dwelling on an island joined to the mainland by a guarded bridge. The downside to being one of the most successful military leaders of your time is you may have accrued many enemies along the way."

Seeking permission to land had been surprisingly easy and Jenni was suspicious of the reason why. Their craft had been sent directions and a pass-code to use when disembarking.

"It all seems too easy," Jenni said to Hamen as they alighted from the confines of the small ship.

Each stretched their tight muscles as they stood surveying the hanger they now found themselves in. What struck Jenni most about their location was the lushness of the vegetation. It climbed up the walls of the hanger and weaved in and out of the machinery. Vinelike tendrils covered the roof giving the illusion of being in a tropical forest.

"Welcome to my corner of the universe," a booming voice called across the vast space of the hanger.

A giant figure strode towards them, flanked by two equally enormous companions. Jenni took in the details of his appearance. She had many friends who were Sringey or part Sringey, but none had the overbearing presence of the one who now faced her. His long dark hair covered most of his face and body, shortening at his protruding snout. His bright amber eyes seemed to feast on Hamen, hardly glancing in her direction at all. The elongated fangs which held a deadly poison were nestled in the gums, but Jenni had seen enough of the race to know, if riled, those weapons would extend to full capacity right down past the chin. The muscled flanks of his legs were exposed as was the rest of his taut body. Only a small skin cloth, wrapped around his waist, covered the impressive frame.

"Many thanks indeed for your courtesy," Hamen responded, bowing low in a gesture of respect. "Your courage is famed across the universe as is your generosity."

Jenni nodded her agreement, knowing enough about the Sringey to understand she could not speak unless she had been addressed directly.

"I am honored to be visited by a Trinz," The General's eyes gleamed as he indentified Hamen. "There is much we could learn from your race if you would only share your wisdom."

"As we once did, we will do no more," Hamen spoke sadly the words of his people.

"So be it," the General closed the topic. "Now, introduce me to your human companion. Quite a delightful pet!"

"This is Jenni and I am Hamen. We seek assistance and wish to exchange vessels to continue our journey."

"All in good time," the General said, his voice had returned to its magnificent boom. "Come, rest yourselves and partake of my hospitality. We will feast and you can tell me your tale."

Leading the way, the General headed out of the hanger. His men walked rather menacingly behind Hamen and Jenni, giving them no choice but to comply.

"Tell him nothing," Hamen hissed as they emerged into the fresh air.

Jenni's reply was replaced by a sigh of wonder as she beheld the splendor around her. Resplendent flowers burst from a sea of greenery. Large fruits hung down, straining to be plucked and savored. An impressive structure stood at the end of an avenue of foliage, its turrets and spires a tribute to gothic extravagance.

"My humble abode," the General gestured with his open arms, the paw-like palms extended up to the lilac sky.

"My guards will take you to a place where you can clean yourselves. I will expect you at the setting of the suns for a time of tales, dining and friendship."

The General disappeared towards the house, leaving Hamen and Jenni to follow the henchmen to a tiny cottage that seemed to grow from among the vines. Pulling back the branchy entrance, Jenni saw a deep pool with two wide beds beside it. Fruit dripped from the overhanging boughs, and the dappled light danced invitingly on the water's surface.

"When in Rome," Jenni giggled, eager to submerge herself in the water.

Hamen frowned at the reference. "Where is Rome?" he asked.

"Earth, I think," Jenni answered. "It is just a saying. It means we should get in and have some fun."

Hamen watched as Jenni stripped off her clothes and discarded them in a careless pile at her feet. She stepped towards the water's edge.

"You had better join me in case I slip," she flirted coyly.

Hamen did as she had, although he laid his clothes neatly folded on the foot of the bed. Hand in hand they stepped in together then ducked down so the water concealed their nakedness. Heads bobbing on the surface, they faced one another. For a long moment their eyes held fast as if drinking in the sight that met them.

Hamen reached for her spare hand and clasped it in his own. He pulled her forward, never taking his eyes from hers. Jenni felt the hard length of his body and wrapped her legs around his waist. The buoyancy held her close to him as her lips moved towards his.

Jenni moaned as Hamen responded to her brazen kiss. His mouth slanted over hers again and again claiming her with possessive fury.

"There will be no meeting of men on your return," he growled into her. "You are mine."

The finality in his words sent a pulse racing to Jenni's core. The heat pooled between her legs despite the cool water.

"Make me yours now," Jenni invited. She pulled her hand from his and reached down to guide him into her. She was more than ready to take him and did so totally.

Lifting herself up against his body, Jenni slid up then back down, sliding up and down his heavy erection. Her breasts rubbed against his chest then up to his waiting mouth. He captured them and tongued their peaks, sending delightful waves of pleasure through her body. Jenni's movement became more frenzied. She could feel the friction of the rough hair between his legs rubbing against her with merciless pressure.

"Oh yes!" Jenni cried.

Her hands wrapped themselves in his thick hair, and she pulled his head closer to her bouncing breasts. Hamen cupped her rear as her pulled her tighter against him. He guided them to the edge of the pool then, effortlessly, lifted her out and laid her on the edge. Rising above her, water cascading from his body, Hamen thrust himself deeper into her. His hips ground against her before he pulled out and sank back down, filling her with his manhood.

Jenni could feel the pressure building. It was time and she cried out her delight. Her head jerked from side to side as the pulsing overtook her. She could feel her core gripping him as her pleasure exploded.

"Jenni!" Hamen grunted as his ecstasy joined with hers and they met as one; united in their passion.

As easily as if she were a child, Hamen lifted Jenni to the downy softness of the bed. Together they reclined, naked in each other's arms. Hearts pounding, they each tried to regain control of their sated bodies.

"You are mine," Hamen reiterated the point after a few quiet minutes. "That Yosi has no claim on you."

Jenni smiled a slow smile. "Mmmmm!" she agreed. "Yours."

Her eyes closed as sleep claimed her; her head on a pillow of hard male flesh.

~ * ~

Hamen heard the regularity of Jenni's breathing and knew she had fallen asleep. He enjoyed seeing slumber take her so readily after their lovemaking. What he hadn't enjoyed so much was the flirty exchange he had heard between Jenni and Yosi. She had spoken in such a throaty voice that he had wanted to rip right through the metal casing and tear the man limb from limb. Hamen knew enough about human emotion to know he was experiencing jealousy. He had studied humans as part of his initiation into the Killanti Project. Despite that, he had never felt anything that made him feel so vulnerable and sick deep within.

The Trinz had bred any such emotion out of their systems in the laboratories where their babies were given life. The weakness of emotion was blamed for many of the mistakes in the history of the Trinz as well as being recognized as the underlying fault of humankind. It was impossible for him to be experiencing such feelings but undeniable that he was. More determined than ever to get to the heart of the mystery, Hamen turned his attention to the Sringey.

He had heard of the General. Who hadn't? His military genius was renowned across the universe. He was also rumored to aspire to the knowledge of the Trinz. Many ambitious individuals attempted to infiltrate the Trinz over the years, yearning for the knowledge of the universe that eluded them. General T. Goaf was one of them. The Trinz never concerned themselves much with the Sringey. Their minds were too primitive to be of use and their dreams revolved around more primitive pursuits such as hunting and mating. Combat was their strength and it was not a skill the Trinz valued for their utopist world of Killanti.

Hamen was concerned they may not be free to depart from this planet. He would need to spin a convincing yarn without revealing too much of the truth. The Sringey thrived on oral representation of events. They cared not for the human form of written communication, preferring instead to pass messages on through word of mouth and storytelling. A visitor would be expected to tell his tale in exchange for food and lodgings, passing on tales of what he or she had heard whilst traveling. If the tale were informative enough for the host, the guest would then be honored by the host's own tale, which would then be taken to the next planet or "port of call" by the travelers. It generally worked well for the Sringey but had led to some misunderstandings throughout their volatile history. Whole clan groups had been wiped out due to elaborated retellings of tales. Rival clans had entered bitter disputes that lasted generations thanks to a meddlesome messenger omitting details from their telling. Hamen had to be smart. He lay with his arm around Jenni and set about spinning his own yarn.

Chapter Seven

A gentle kiss woke Jenni from her dreamless sleep. Hamen's damp hair curled around his face.

"You went in again without me," Jenni complained petulantly as her fingers touched his wet hair.

"Seemed the best way to avoid distraction," Hamen said honestly. "The suns begin to set and the sky is darkening to indigo. We must head up to dine with the General. He will be expecting us."

Hamen spoke the truth. As soon as Jenni had redressed herself, the branches that concealed them parted and the burley guards from before stood ready to escort them.

The General was seated on a pillow at a low table laden with plates of food. The fruits were fresh and the meat was raw. Jenni noticed a rusty colored female next to him. Her long snout was elegant and her hair was smoothed flat against her sleek body.

"My mate, Fixa," The General explained. "This is Jenni and Hamen," he added to his companion.

Hamen and Jenni bobbed their heads as they responded to The General's gesture and sat at the opposite side of the table. Hamen's plate was soon piled up with fruits, and he tucked in hungrily to the fare. Jenni tasted a little more cautiously but was soon enjoying the sweet nectar of the orange fleshed fruit.

"I see you both like our local delicacy," Fixa purred. "It is our best kept secret. We engineered it to grow here. It is the only place in the universe you can taste its sweetness. My mate likes to own unique things," she added with a low growl of desire.

"I do," The General replied. "That is why I am so fascinated by a Trinz in a human vessel turning up on my planet and asking for docking so far from the human base. I am sure you can see why my interest is aroused."

The general leaned forward as if greedy to know their story. Jenni swallowed and looked to Hamen

This was all his, she decided.

"As with your own great race," Hamen began courteously, paying his respects to the attributes of the Sringey through his carefully woven words. "The Trinz have also observed and aimed to guide the human race in its growth. Just as parent cares for its young so we elder races have tried to nurture the growth of the primitive races."

Jenni turned a scowl at Hamen as he, once again, managed to insult her people. Hamen ignored her stare and continued with his prose.

"I know your ancestor Anubis set out many thousands of years ago, along with representatives from throughout the universe, with the aim of forging bonds to culture and guide the human race."

Anubis, Jenni's eyes widened as she recalled her school History class and the hieroglyphic chip she had rented from the school data base. She recalled a jackal-headed god that had been significant in the early civilizations on Earth. Hamen shot her a glance filled with warning and she, sensibly, remained quiet as Hamen continued.

"The Trinz seek now to guide the humans back to ways that would bring harmony to the universe again. We seek to find liked minded humans from among the many to culture a new species. Paradises like yours need not be so few and far between," Hamen appeared to be feeding The General honeyed words to lull him into aiding their mission. "We seek a fellow Trinz who resides far from here. We ask to exchange our craft for one less, well, less obvious and we seek safe passage to leave with fuel and supplies for our quest. The human girl has many of the qualities each of our kind once saw in the humans. Qualities we can nourish once more!"

By the end of the tirade, Jenni got the distinct impression Hamen was quite enjoying himself. His face was flushed and his arms were moving in flamboyant circles. Jenni looked towards his audience and noticed their rapt attention.

They're buying it, she marveled.

"I concur that it would be beneficial to acquire the technology found on a human craft. Their food simulation system interests me greatly. If I agree to your terms, I ask that you mention nothing of what you have seen here or give away my location. Many races still bear grudges towards the Sringey, and I live here in peace."

"Let us agree to trade then," Hamen bowed low before the wolf-like creature. "Our mutual silence regarding this encounter and a trade of vessel."

"Agreed."

The rest of the evening passed with relative speed. The food was fresh and delicious and the company was entertaining. Each told his or her own tale of beginning, including from where they came to how they got to the place they found themselves. Jenni was most enthralled by Fixa's tale. Hers was a story of rescue from a doomed planet by a brave soldier who went on to be the most influential general in the Sringey militia. Her standing as princess in her own land made her a prize indeed for the ambitious warrior.

Hamen told of a clinical world where children were selected much like a household appliance and demonstrations of love seemed to be withheld from the young. Jenni shared a tale of love, laughter and sorrow. She was pleased The General had heard of her parents and the sorrow he expressed at their passing seemed genuine and heartfelt.

When Hamen and Jenni were shown to their beds, the pair sank into an exhausted sleep curled tight in each other's arms.

It was in the early hours of morning when Jenni awoke from her slumber. A sound outside her room startled her. As her eyes opened, the sound repeated itself. It was as if a bird called for its mate; over and over again the cry could be heard. Jenni pulled herself to her feet and walked to the leafy voile that covered the entrance to the room. Outside, in the half light of dawn, Jenni was surprised to see a figure dart behind a tree in front of her. The shadowy appearance of the croft made her unsure as to what manner of creature it was.

As she watched, an arm extended from behind the textured bark and beckoned her closer. Jenni stepped towards the tree, her natural inquisitiveness pervading her common sense. A hand stopped her before she had taken her second step.

"Where are you going?" hissed Hamen, his voice so close to her ear that she could feel his breath on her neck.

"Someone called to me," she answered. "I came out to see and someone moved behind that tree. I was going to find out just what they wanted."

"And what of your safety?" Hamen's voice was soft but laced with anger.

"I didn't really give it much thought," Jenni admitted.

"We'll go together," Hamen said more kindly.

Hand in hand they rounded the tree. No soul was in sight. Jenni looked around to see if the figure was camouflaged among the greenery. A slight movement caught her eye and she gestured to Hamen. He nodded and they moved slowly towards the flicker.

"We are friends," Jenni called out. "Can we help you?"

As they watched, a small furry figure came out from behind the tree. Its dark face and elongated muzzle made Jenni certain it was a young Sringey, most likely belonging to The General and Fixa judging by the rusty color of his fur.

"Hello, there," Jenni cooed. "Aren't you a fine looking boy?"

The gentle tone of her voice seemed to strike a chord with the youngling. He took hold of her hand and pulled her through the trees to a locked out building. The boy started around the back and pulled Jenni after him. Jenni, in turn, grabbed Hamen's hand and the three of them entered a side door into the building.

Hamen's hand gripped hers as they stopped and stared at a pill shaped container that lay in the middle of the room.

"It can't be!" Hamen exclaimed.

"What can't it be?" Jenni asked, alarmed by the note of terror in Hamen's voice.

"Killanti," Hamen added.

"The place? What do you mean?" Jenni was confused.

The hairy boy looked from one adult to the other. His furry brow was corrugated as if puzzled by the exchange.

"The machine is a Trinz design. I know because it is almost identical to the one I lay in night after night when I came to you in your dreams. The question is what is it doing here? It must have come from the first wave; the one that went wrong."

"You are correct," a voice boomed from the door. The general stood with the youngling grasped firmly in his paw. "As I said, I like to acquire things. This was a welcome addition or it would be if it worked. Maybe you can tinker with it a little."

"What do you know of its use?" Hamen asked.

"Oh, I know all about the Killanti Project," The General said. "I have made it my business to find out, and I had a visitor here once, around twenty-five years ago now, who filled me in on many aspects of the project. He left this in exchange for my help. Let's just say that he wanted some help to disappear."

"I seek this man," Hamen said.

"You do and by the way you look at the human, I suspect you have found yourself in the position that ended the first Killanti Project. I would pay many credits to discover the secret of mind travel and many more to find out how a connected mind is able to transport a body across the universe."

"I wish I knew," Hamen said ruefully. "I could save myself a great deal of trouble if I knew the answer."

"It seems I have come close again only to have the secret elude me. What I can do is prevent you from a wild goose chase. Any information you think you have on the one you seek will lead you to a dead end. He has covered his trail well. I can give you the coordinates of the planet where he resides."

'Why would you help us?" Jenni asked.

"I do ask a small thing in return. I ask to see Killanti. Take me there."

"That I cannot promise," Hamen said. "Killanti is a place few have seen. I have never been privy to the location. I can only vow to try my best to include you in the short list."

"That vow I will take," The General agreed. "Now, come let me show you to your craft."

Stopping briefly to gather their things, Hamen and Jenni followed The General back to his private hanger.

In the place where their ship had landed the day before stood a different craft. It was bigger but a much older model. Its battered facade gave the impression it had been through some meteor showers or bruised in battle.

"She's more than she looks," a smaller, grey Sringey spoke as they approached. "She'll serve you well."

"Thank you," Hamen and Jenni spoke as one.

"I will hold you to your vow and hope to see you back here," The General said with a voice as hard as granite.

"I will do my best," Hamen said.

On board the ship, Jenni could not fail to be impressed with the technology. The ship was what was known as a cover vessel. Its shabby exterior deterred any potential bandits from coveting its wealth. Screens surrounded the small cockpit with the touch sensitive technology to navigate the vessel with hand movements only. Jenni quickly settled into her seat, reclined and adjusted it to enable her to reach the screens. She turned to catch Hamen staring at her with a dark glint in his eyes.

"Yes?" she smiled slowly.

"I was just admiring the way you handle your equipment," he said with a roguish grin.

"Oh, were you now?" Jenni fluttered her eyelashes as she looked up at him.

"If you look at me like that, we may not take off from this planet."

"Oh no! We must get away from here," Jenni urged.

"Agreed!" All business now, Hamen sat down and arranged his own screens.

"Coordinates in?" he asked.

"Check." replied Jenni.

"Let's get out of here," Hamen added as the engine sprang into life.

"I'll see you on Jamaica 2," Hamen promised with a heavy wink.

"Not if I see you first!" Jenni retorted tartly.

Chapter Eight

On Jamaica 2, Timon woke up and stretched out his long limbs. The bed sagged under the weight of the giant man. At the door a woman leaned casually on the frame. Her eyes were alight with love as she watched her man awaken.

"Don't just stand there with those come to bed eyes. Just come to bed," he growled.

Hope stood there longer, the smile that was playing on her lips widening to light up her whole face. Her ebony skin contrasted with the brilliant white of her perfect teeth. Timon was insatiable. Hope knew if she didn't comply, her would leap up and carry her to the bed himself. She could see by the tenting in the single sheet that he was fully awake and ready to indulge his appetite once more. Hope slowly untied the sarong she had wrapped loosely around her waist and let it fall to the floor. Her exposed, ample breasts swayed with the movement and her hips swung provocatively as she sashayed to the bed. Keeping her eyes on the man who ogled her, she closed the gap between them and gave herself up for his pleasure.

She recalled the first time she and Timon had met. He had arrived on Jamaica 2 and stayed at her grandmother's hostel. Hope had been working there as she had just completed her studies and was awaiting her first appointment on a bio-transporter. Timon had seemed lost somehow, despite his giant size. He was mysterious and totally disinterested in Hope apart from being a source of information on the planet and its surrounding area.

As a sexually promiscuous young woman, Hope was confused by the lack of physical interest he displayed towards her. Despite her best efforts to bend down low over his table or swing her generous hips as she passed, Timon remained oblivious to her charms. Hope finally concluded he was uninterested in females at all and sought to introduce him to a male friend of hers whom she was sure he would desire.

Jarvain was tall and smoothed skinned and had a lean appearance that belied his muscular form. Jarvain, it seemed was not at all Timon's type, and the boy had almost suffered a beating had it not been for Hope's last minute intervention. As they sat side by side after the incident, Timon had confided he was a Trinz. He explained their aversion to physical contact after a nasty virus had almost wiped out their species. The sexually transmitted plague had forced the elders to outlaw sexual activity. Generations had bred the urge out of the race, and partnerships had become completely about companionship and mutual respect.

Hope recalled her attempt to corrupt the stranger. It had become quite a game to her and finally culminated in a passionate clinch that led to Timon's first sexual experience. Hope had unleashed a beast. Tomin's insatiable desire for her had caused her to remain on the planet and work at a local bio-dome. Together they were cocooned in a blissful paradise of erotic fulfilment.

Looking down at him now as she rode him gently to their mutual satisfaction, Hope praised again the fates that had conspired to bring Timon to her world. She dreaded the day she knew would come; when he decided to return to his world or was sought out by his own kind. Hope was not stupid; she knew he was running. His manner each and every time a new vessel docked was evidence enough. Then his relief when the ship was bound for a different purpose brought a pain to Hope's kind heart.

~ * ~

Just as the pair screamed out their ecstatic climax, a loud rap on the door brought Timon crashing from his wave of desire. For the umpteenth time, he cursed his kind for denying him such pleasure for so long. Hope had educated him in so many delicious ways, and he wanted her in so many different ways over and over again throughout the day. Even when she was away from him, he craved and fantasized about her dark, silky skin and musky scent. The door knocking was an unwelcome interruption to his morning satisfaction and he shouted expletives gruffly at the closed metal door.

Using his finger to activate the sensor, Timon was surprise to see a startled boy standing outside. His wide eyes seemed to take in the rumpled bed and the disheveled woman who was barely concealed in a sheet. Timon stood before him like a naked giant in all his sated glory.

"Well? This better be good, boy," Timon bellowed at the trembling lad.

"I...you...you told me to come if any ships came from Columbia 2. One has just docked," the boy stuttered.

Timon's blood ran cold. He knew the trail would reach him one day. He had trusted the Sringey on Columbia 2 about as much as he'd trust a snarling dog, but he had hoped the trade he had made would buy The General's silence.

"I am on my way," Timon barked, already moving through the room and pulling on his garments. His work attire was an overall style zipped fronted trouser suit. It served to protect him from the grime of the repair shop which he had bought soon after his arrival on Jamaica 2. His knowledge of machines and of the advanced technology of the Trinz had soon established him as a miracle worker. Old gadgets that seemed redundant were given a lease of life and ships were granted upgrades well beyond what their worn out shells should achieve.

Timon's long legs soon transported him to the edge of the docking bay. He was in time to see a tall young man with a younger female escort. Timon recognized the boy at once as a Trinz. It puzzled him that he was accompanied by a human girl and if they had come for him, why there were only two of them in one of The General's old war crafts? Timon watched as one of the docking officers nodded and turned, pointing and waving in his direction.

"Damn," Timon cursed as the Trinz turned his face towards him.

Eye contact established, Timon was forced to raise his hand in a greeting and wait until the younger man had closed the distance between them.

Timon balked as the obvious Trinz-like features came into focus.

"I was expecting more of a consort when they finally caught up with me," Timon said ruefully.

"I am not here on official Trinz business. I am Hamen and I am seeking one who may know something of the first wave of the Killanti Project. This is Jenni," he added with no elaboration about the girl.

Timon reached out and grabbed the younger man's arm. "Not here," he hissed. "Come with me."

The trio marched away from the docking port and into a smaller shed across a wooden slatted bridge that crossed a clear blue stream nestled among some large tropical ferns. The high doors swung open as Timon pulled the rope handle and motioned them inside. He pulled up a couple of dirty, oil covered stools and indicated for them to sit. He then proceeded to a battered fridge and pulled out three bottles of water. The caps were removed and Hamen and Jenni drank thirstily.

"I have been here so many years without discovery. How is it a lone Trinz and his human pet have arrived knowing my whereabouts?"

"Jenni is my companion," Hamen said with an edge to his voice. "We arranged a deal with The General. He told us where to find you. I need your help," Hamen added more humbly. Then looking towards Jenni, he added, "We need your help."

"I'm listening," Timon said, pulling up a stool for himself and settling onto it. He started swigging his water down in large, noisy gulps.

Timon's hand soon stilled as he listened to the tale Hamen told. His water seemed suspended in mid air as Hamen explained about the second Killanti Project and how he had joined with Jenni the night she had slipped into the pool. Timon's mind raced. He recalled a similar story that had been the reason the first wave of the Killanti Project failed and why he was stranded on the other side of the universe.

Timon began to visualize the scene that had happened so many years ago. He had arrived early to help release the Trinz volunteers from their telekinetic chambers. The young recruits, known as the Communers, were often disorientated and needed to debrief after their "contact." Timon was strongly opposed to the way the Elder Panel showed no regard for the well being of the young people whose intelligence and aptitude for mind control had brought them to the attention of the panel. Each day, they were required to connect to the mind of a carefully chosen human and use their influence to draw them to the paradise world of Killanti. Once there, the Trinz would mold and educated them into a better and more sustainable way of living. Timon had visited the planet once. It was indeed a haven of peace and abundant life. The atmosphere suited both the human and the Trinz race, and no biospheres were needed. Dwellings had grown into villages and the population had multiplied. New Killantians were proud of their world and served to preserve the way of life that had been established.

All seemed to have happened according to plan until that one day when Timon came across the trembling figure convulsing on the floor of the Killanti programming base on Trinz. It was evident to Timon the man was human. He was the selected human assigned to Rein; a prodigy of the Trinz who was destined for higher things within the Elder Panel. Rein had been having some unusual readings for the last few weeks, and Timon had been charged with discovering more about her connection. Rein was due to be promoted after she secured her latest recruit. Her marriage to Ju, one of the Elder Panel, was her ticket to a more privileged position. Rein lay wired up to the machines, still very much in a state of unconscious.

Timon scooped up the human and carried him to a cell where the atmosphere could be controlled. Summoning a medical professional who could be relied on for his discretion, Timon went in search of Wren, his colleague on the Elder Panel. Wren had insisted the man be sedated and Rein be told nothing of the unfortunate event. Her impending marriage was too important to risk a scandal. Under a controlled mind sweep, it transpired that the human, Cal, and Rein had been sexually involved. This connection had somehow been strong enough to draw him through the universe in a teleportal stream.

Timon shuddered as he remembered the passion the man had shown when he was finally allowed to gain back his own conscious mind. He yearned for the woman he had fallen in love with; a woman who had no knowledge of his existence on Trinz. Timon had been given the task of telling Rein her mission had ended successfully and Cal had safely reached Killanti. Her eyes had betrayed her emotion as they welled with tears. Timon recalled the way she had straightened her back and nodded.

"That is that then," she said as she turned and left to take up her new role as Elder and embark on her marriage.

The injustice of the situation bothered Timon and he approached Wren about it. Wren promptly stripped him of his rank and publicly disgraced him in society. It was Timon who had been blamed for the demise of the Killanti Project. He had been held accountable for the faulty machines and the danger to the participants. Wren released news of the tragic deaths of the human participants, claiming the mind tools had been too potent for the inferior human brain. Timon was forced to flee the planet thus guaranteeing his silence and ensuring his credibility held no worth. Managing to secure a pod for bargaining, Timon left Trinz.

Now, here was this young Trinz informing him that another had passed through the universe. Drawn, it would seem, by the same level of attraction. Timon mused about the similarity. He vowed to find out more about the visitors who sought him out. This was a mystery he fully intended to solve.

Chapter Nine

Jenni watched the interplay between the two men. She saw how the big man sat up higher in his seat when Hamen explained how he found himself in Jenni's bed. Jenni blushed under his scrutiny as Hamen explained how they connected in the dream realm and how they had established a physical relationship. Timon listened. Then, when Hamen had completed his story, he began to ask questions. He asked about Hamen, who his parents were and how he had come to be working for the Elder Panel. He bombarded Jenni with questions of her own parentage and her position aboard Chicago 3. He asked who had known of the initial contact and what they had advised. Finally, he wanted to know who knew about his own presence on Jamaica 2.

Seemingly satisfied with Hamen and Jenni's answers, Timon suggested they return to his home for some lunch. They realized they had been talking for hours and the rumbling of their stomachs told them it was time to eat. They followed the massive giant of a man out of the workshop and along a narrow series of woodened walkways. Jenni could not help but stop and admire the flora and fauna. Its lush green canopy was causing a dappled glow to the pathways.

"Quite something, isn't it?" Timon said quietly.

"It really is," Jenni breathed. "It looks like the place I dreamed of."

She looped her arm into Hamen's and looked up at him.

"Killanti," he replied smiling down at her.

"Come and meet my Hope," Timon's voice interrupted their moment. "She is human too," he turned to Jenni. "I think you'll like her."

"I am sure I will," Jenni said.

Timon's house was covered in vines which, in turn, were hung with a rich crimson flower. The stone construction seemed to be verging on the derelict, but its homely feel compensated for the disrepair. A dark skinned woman threw open the door and beamed at them.

"Greetings to you all," she welcomed them. "Come in and have some refreshment. I do so like visitors."

"Thank you," Hamen and Jenni chorused.

Inside the house vibrant colors adorned the walls and furnishings. Large low seating was scattered with colorful cushions in hues of red and green.

"Sit and eat," Hope invited as she entered the room with a tray of tall glasses topped with ice. Timon followed with a platter of fresh fruit.

After introductions had been made, the group tucked in. Juices dribbled down their chins as the conversation flowed freely. Hope told of her carefree upbringing, and Timon filled her in on the adventures of Hamen and Jenni. Hope marveled at the romance of their story whilst Timon remained pensive. Jenni noticed the way his gaze often settled upon Hamen as if he were trying to see something or seek an answer to a question.

"Your mother, her name is Rein?" he asked at last.

"It is," Hamen replied. "Do you know her?"

"Yes, I do. I worked with her during the first Killanti Project. She was pulled into the Elder Panel just before the first wave came to an end. What do you know of her involvement?"

"I just know she was not keen at all for me to get involved. It took my father and Wren to convince her."

"I bet they were very persuasive," Timon snarled. "You should never have been included. I do not know what they were thinking."

"What do you mean?" Hamne argued. "You sound like my mother."

"Judging by your age and some of your features, I suspect you were born of a human father," Timon spoke candidly. "Your mother faced a situation much like your own. I was a part of the conspiracy that covered up the truth. It would have ruined the Project; something that was not an option for the Trinz. Killanti is so much more than one anomaly."

"Anomaly!" Hamen raged. "My mother is a well-respected member of the Elders. She would not have been party to such a cover up."

"Loyalty is a fine characteristic," Timon praised. "Your mother had no knowledge of the breach. She believed that, like you, she had made contact with a human in the dream realm. One morning I found a human on the floor of her mind chamber. He was removed before she knew anything about it. She was betrothed to your father. It was a match that suited the Elder Panel."

"And the human?" Hamen asked.

"That I do not know," Timon admitted. "Cal was his name. You have a look of him. It is why I suspect you may have been born in the old way. It may be why you could also transport."

"Interesting," Hamen said.

"Interesting?" Jenni blurted out. "You have just been told you may have a human father and all you can say is 'interesting'."

"Biological parents are not relevant to me," Hamen explained. "Trinz never know who provides the egg or sperm. We are just implanted into host mothers then collected by our true parents on delivery. It is the way of things for us."

Timon nodded in agreement although Jenni saw the frown crease Hope's smooth brow.

"What do you want of me?" Timon continued, returning to the purpose of the visit.

"We wish you to help us find Killanti," Jenni interjected. "It is where we will live together."

"Ah!" Timon said with understanding. "I see. You wish me to give you the coordinates."

"We do," Hamen added. "It is a secret to all but the chosen. I was not at the stage with the Project to give the coordinates to Jenni. Many Trinz seek to dwell there, but only the select few are sent. The coordinates are a state secret."

"It is as it should be," Timon said sagely. "Trinz is a very strict planet. There are many who would seek to migrate to a new planet; a place where the rules are freer. Killanti must be monitored if it is to succeed."

"It sounds as if much has been sacrificed for this planet," Hope noted. "Although I expect there is no such thing as the perfection your kind seeks."

"Maybe you are right," Timon reached for her hand and gave it a squeeze. "I have certainly found my perfection here."

Jenni smiled at the pair. She turned to look at Hamen who was staring at her with smoldering dark eyes. Jenni's skin prickled under his gaze. Color flushed to her cheeks and her stomach turned over in anticipation.

"If you two will excuse us," Timon spoke without taking his eyes off of Hope.

Without waiting for a response, they disappeared through another door, already undressing each other with hungry eyes.

Hamen's own eyes now extended an invitation that made Jenni's heart race.

"Shall we look around outside?" she suggested. "It seems to suit us."

"Indeed it does," Hamen said with an intimate tone. "Come."

He slipped his hand into hers and led her out of the front door and into the verdant surroundings. A winding path led off in the opposite direction from where they had come earlier. It led through a narrow gate and along the edge of a patchwork of fields that stretched as far as the eye could see. The fields were filled with yellow crops that moved gracefully in the gentle breeze. The sun seemed large in the sky due to its close proximity to the planet.

"It is more than three quarters through its life," Jenni said indicating the fiery globe. "Perfect conditions for life though not for many more generations. Jamaica 2 is where much of the oil is produced for human consumption. It has a mellow and rich quality and enhances the flavor of food when cooked."

Jenni felt she may be babbling but she was feeling nervous. It had been a while since she and Hamen had been intimate, and the tension was rife between them. Jenni knew one touch from him would send her into a frenzy of passion, and the thought of it was already making her moist.

"When I was growing up we..." Jenni continued her babbling until firm lips silenced her.

Hamen's arms pulled Jenni closer to him. The pressure of his mouth increased and his forked tongue pushed against her lips, demanding entry. Jenni instantly obliged and welcomed his oral onslaught. Purring in pleasure, she writhed against him, her hips circling into his and relishing the solid bulge she encountered.

Hamen broke the kiss and Jenni heard the sound of his groan.

"This way," he urged, pulling her into the field.

Soon the couple was dwarfed by the tall, sunny crop. It loomed above them and provided a yellow canopy. Hamen pulled her into his embrace and ran his kisses along her neck. Jenni threw back her head and wallowed in the pleasure of his touch. When he reached the place where her neck and shoulders joined, Hamen focused on the hollow dent, making Jenni cry out with desire.

She tried in vain to return the caress, but her senses were overwhelmed and she could do little but moan and pant, already on the precipice of satisfaction. Jenni's incapacity seemed to act as an aphrodisiac to Hamen. The more Jenni whimpered and writhed, the more he maintained his delightful exploration.

Hamen had pulled Jenni's clothing from her body and used it to fashion a makeshift cover for them to lie upon. Side by side they lay facing each other under the yellow tent. Hamen's hands were relentless. They stroked and probed and clawed at Jenni's soft flesh making every nerve ending in her body alive with a tingling sensation.

Jenni lay back upon the softness of her clothing. She gazed up at the floral ceiling and gave herself up the pure bliss of Hamen's expert hands. Again and again he brought her to the edge of satisfaction only to stop with a cheeky smile.

"Please," Jenni asked over and over again.

"I want to know every part of you," Hamen responded, murmuring teasingly against her skin..

At last, he paused and rose up above her.

"Are you ready?" he growled.

"Yes!" Jenni gasped, watching as he lowered his length towards her.

Filling her with one deep thrust, Jenni knew she was just moments from losing control. She lifted her legs and wrapped them around Hamen's thick torso, pulling him right into her and holding him there.

She began to grind her hips against him, marveling at the friction building inside her.

Hamen bit his lip and threw back his head as he withdrew slightly then buried himself inside her again. The pressure was too much for Jenni, she felt her core tighten and the waves of her orgasm begin. Hamen cried out as he too allowed his control to snap. Together they clung to each other as ecstasy reigned supreme.

Sated, they lay watching the rays of sun that passed through the yellow crops. The vibrant patterns danced across the secluded space that housed them.

"Do you wish to find out if the human man is your father?" Jenni asked.

"Hmm. I will admit to being curious about my heritage," Hamen replied, "although it would mean returning to Trinz to question my parents. That could make things difficult for us."

"In what way?" Jenni asked.

"Humans are prohibited from landing on Trinz. It is the one place that is unavailable to the human race."

Jenni detected the animosity to humans again in his tone. She chose to ignore it, biting down the jibe that he himself may be part human.

"I have a feeling many things may prove difficult for us," Jenni said instead. "It would be good to know why we connected as we did, and I think the answers will be found on Trinz. Maybe I can wait for you back on my ship or on a closer planet."

Jenni wasn't sure if it were the breeze that made her shiver then but she rather suspected it was the thought of being separated from Hamen. In a short space of time, she had come to rely on him.

Hamen pulled her closer as he felt her body shiver. "I hope we can find a way to stay together," he said.

Jenni felt foolish as a wide smile split her face. "That would be good," she whispered.

Chapter Ten

It was dawn on Columbia 2 as the two generals faced each other; each blatantly curious about the other. Neither had ever met, but the reputations of the two fearsome warriors were the most notorious across the whole universe.

"We know they were here," General Lio growled with menace. "The trace of the vessel led us to this point."

"I know nothing of the human you speak of and her Trinz mate. None visit here without my express invitation and I consort with no human, ever." General T. Goaf replied. The scorn in his words made his displeasure in Lio's visit evident.

"Then it seems we are at a stalemate," Lio sneered. He had no intention of leaving this pitiful place without the information he required.

General Lio was furious. Not only had one of his ships been stolen using his name, but he now found a Trinz male had been a stowaway. Lio detested the Trinz. Their elusive presence in the universe and their lofty position in the hierarchy of races left him seeing red. His mission was to seek out their planet and conquer it. It was the sole purpose that drove him to push deeper and deeper into space, colonizing planet after planet. None other would satisfy his lust for power. Within his grasp had been the coordinates to Trinz, and he had lost them.

Lio did not tolerate failure in his militia, and he certainly did not entertain the idea of failure within himself. He had decided to personally deal with the situation. He had been aware of Jenni, her parents had been among his best commanders, and their deaths had been an unfortunate price of progress. He had earmarked Jenni to be the lead navigator on his next mission to the unchartered Yankee Zone. Lio was hopeful the new galaxy would reap the reward of housing the planet the Trinz called home. He was not getting any younger and his need for revenge was raw.

As the two, equally stubborn, generals sized each other up, a young officer approached General Lio. He leaned forward and whispered into his commander's ear. Lio's face broke into a sneer of victory. He looked triumphantly towards General T. Goaf.

"It seems my young officer here has located my missing ship."

"That is not possible," General Goaf spluttered.

"Oh, it was almost unrecognizable," Lio continued smugly. "There is a tracer we have been working on, rather like a DNA identifier. It works to locate lost machinery. It is a constant problem with the human race being so diversely spread across the universe. This device read the carbon trace of a vessel and forms an identification tag, of sorts."

Goaf paled as Lio stepped forward, sensing his imminent victory.

"Jamaica 2," he mumbled. "They took one of my ships and went to Jamaica 2."

"Get a trace of the vessel from the docking bays," Lio ordered, already making for his warship. "Kill him," he hissed to the officer beside him who nodded at his order.

Lio did not look back. He had not risen into the position he had by regretting what was necessary. Goaf knew too much. Many would seek a rogue Trinz, what they knew was worth a life or two along the way.

As Lio walked back onto his vessel, his men lowered their heads and busied themselves with the tasks needed for takeoff. He was feared and obeyed but not liked, and that suited him well enough. His face broke into an evil smile as the thrum of the engines vibrated through him. He was hot on the trail of the Trinz, and he had the element of surprise on his side. Having the upper hand was just the way General Lio liked it to be.

Chapter Eleven

The days passed idyllically for Jenni and Hamen. They spent time together as well as time with Timon and Hope. Together, they poured over maps of the universe trying to ascertain the location of Killanti. Timon knew the route from Trinz, but the secret coordinates of Trinz were never shared with any of its race of inhabitants. It was a way of protecting its citizens if they ever ventured around the universe. Only upon their return was the location transmitted to them.

Jenni was baffled by the secrecy. She knew humans had not come close to the location of Trinz, and it was in none of the Zones they had colonized. It therefore followed that it lay between the Yankee and Zulu Zones and it was only a matter of time until it was discovered. Her logic fell on deaf ears though as she spoke to the stubborn Trinz men.

Hope and Jenni spent much time collecting ingredients and cooking up new recipes. Jenni had few female confidants over the years, and she relished the time spent with the Jamaican woman. Hope had inherited the tales and traditions of her ancestors. Generations passed down tales of the old ways and how life on Earth had sustained its people. Many of the recipes were crude yet the flavors were delicious and fresh. Jenni loved how food could be combined and cooked to allow the natural tastes to fuse together. As they worked, Hope regaled Jenni with the stories of her family and the secrets of sustaining what grows around you. In turn, Jenni confessed the details of the land of her dreams and how she longed for a life there.

"You would be happy there," Hope encouraged her. "I sense unease in you for the life of space travel. It is not what your soul strives for. Maybe that is the reason Hamen sought you out from the other side of the universe."

"Maybe," Jenni agreed. "I still find it very hard to grasp how our souls could join through dreams and he could come to me physically."

"The Trinz are older than the universe we know. They have evolved so they can do much that our human minds cannot comprehend. It is well to trust. Your faith must be blind, but it is faith you need. True love remains the strongest force in the universe. It is not the subject of legend and fairytale for nothing. Love should never be underestimated."

Hope's words lingered in Jenni's mind. She had such innocence, yet wisdom was present in her observations. Jenni vowed to let fate lead her to her destiny.

Fate, it seemed, was ready to take a hand in Jenni's life. The next day dawned bright and also brought news that a human warship had docked over night. Hamen and Timon had left early to check it out, rather suspecting it was a quick refueling stop.

Jenni waited for his return under the soft cover that lay on her ample bed. She stretched out lazily as she recalled the times she had spent here filled with passion and new heights of gratification. Hamen's need to know all the pleasures denied him, made for long languid nights. In the anonymity that darkness brings, Hamen told Jenni of his visit to the den of vice that existed on Trinz. Jenni was not surprised to hear an element of the planet still craved the sins of the flesh. She had been delighted by Hamen's appetite and knew, if awakened, other Trinz would certainly have the same needs.

As she waited, Jenni grew more anxious. She was sure Hamen would have returned by now but no sight or sound of him had materialized. Jenni pulled on her clothes that had been hastily discarded in a heap the previous night. Crumpled and fretful, she called a brief farewell to Hope before heading off toward the hanger.

No sign of a docked vessel was in evidence. Jenni approached the silent building with trepidation. Something felt wrong. The place was too quiet. Not even the young men who maintained and repaired the small fleet of vessels used to patrol the planet were there. Usually the blare of their music or the sound of their jovial banter filled the cavernous building. Today, only the sounds of the tropical birds that gathered in the surrounding trees could be heard, and even they seemed subdued as if danger lurked imminently close by.

Undeterred by the warning signs, Jenni pushed open the heavy hanger doors and called out.

"Hamen! Timon!"

No reply was forthcoming. Jenni pressed on into the giant shed. She caught a muffled sound and at the same time glimpsed a shoed foot protruding from behind a long desk.

"Hamen? Timon?" Jenni repeated.

Her voice trailed off as she peered around the desk and saw the prostrate form of Timon. His head was cut and a pool of blood had spilled, haloing around his head.

"No!" Jenni cried as she bent to lift the heavy head onto her lap.

Timon murmured louder and tried to open his eyes. "Hamen," he croaked, "they took him."

"Who took him?" Jenni asked, her voice rising in terror. "Tell me!"

Timon coughed as he tried to continue.

"Lio," he said. "They called him Lio."

"Lio," Jenni cursed. "Will that monster never stop plaguing me?"

She sat back on her heels and rocked Timon gently in her arms. "Where have they taken him?" she said more to herself than to the injured man before her.

A banging sound drew Jenni's attention to the room behind her. The sound was coming through a closed door. Jenni lowered Timon back down, tucking her jacket under his head for support. The wound looked swollen, but Jenni decided it would heal. He seemed to have no further damage. Jenni got up and followed the sound to a locked door. The key had been tossed to one side, and Jenni quickly retrieved it and inserted it into the lock. The door sprung open to reveal the dusky skinned youths who worked in the hanger. Their white teeth flashed in recognition as they faced their rescuer.

"Timon is injured, one of you go for help," Jenni instructed.

The smallest of the group scampered off.

"Did any of you see or hear anything?" Jenni asked.

"Only Lio asking Hamen to show him the way to Trinz. He said he would keep him until he could reveal the coordinates. Said he had ways of extracting the information," one of the lads recalled.

"He does not know it," Jenni objected, more to herself than to the group. "I must go after them."

Returning back to where Timon was now being lifted onto a stretcher, Jenni approached Hope who had heard the commotion and followed the medics. She wrung her hands as she watched the pain flash across Timon's face.

"I must follow them," Jenni said. "I must try to reason with Lio and protect Hamen and his world. The Killanti Project seems to be our best hope for the future. It is a better way to unite and live in harmony with the universe. It cannot be jeopardized."

"Yes, go," Hope urged her new friend. "You have the strength it will take. I see it in you."

The two embraced as friends do, each clinging to the other a little longer than was necessary. Jenni felt a wrench when she finally let go. She faced uncertainty and already yearned for the peace she had found on Jamaica 2.

Chapter Twelve

On board his fighter vessel, General Lio was feeling quite smug. It had been easy to secure the prisoner. He had practically walked right into him upon landing. Lio recognized the two Trinz at once. They seemed to have an ethereal quality about them that set them apart from humans despite their anatomic similarities. Lio wasted no time in ordering the men to be overpowered. Surprise on his side, seizing the smaller man had been easy. The group who tried to come to the aid of the Trinz were soon disposed of and secured in a holding room. Lio cared not if the man he had personally coshed lived or died. Within minutes of landing on the planet, Lio departed it. He regretted not securing the human girl too but knew, if she had even the smallest traits from either of her parents, she would soon be in hot pursuit. Lio couldn't help but be rather thrilled at the prospect of the meeting. He would, of course, have the upper hand, knowing she would attempt a rescue.

Lio turned his attention to the prisoner. He traversed the corridors to the secure cells at the rear of the vessel. Being a warship it was well equipped with prisoner facilities; row after row of cells lined up over two levels each fitted with a secured force field to prevent escape. Each prisoner wore a collar that restricted movement. This combination of defence protocols prevented any break out attempts. Sitting in the second cell from the end, Lio found Hamen staring moodily across the space.

"I have come for coordinates," Lio opened without ceremony. "It is time for you to tell me."

"I cannot tell you what I do not know," Hamen replied wearily. "Trinz do not have the knowledge of their location. It is how we remain untouched by the scourge of the universe."

"In my opinion, Trinz have far too high an opinion of themselves," Lio snarled. "I am sure I can extract what I need from you. After all, you left there to unite with Jenni Gravin. You must have some navigational data stored in your brain."

Lio, who was as astute as any predator, noted the flicker in Hamen's eyes. His instincts rarely failed him, and he sensed there was more to the young man in front of him than he first suspected. So many things did not make sense. There were no records or traces of the Trinz aboard Chicago 3. No docking data, no quarantine records or visitor requests. If Lio had not been a realist, he would have concluded Hamen had just appeared there out of the blue. The first and only sign of him had been aboard the stolen ship that left Chicago 3.

"How did you get aboard Chicago 3?" Lio asked. His eyes squinted as he watched for any facial tics or tells.

"I...I...was aboard a cargo shipment," he stammered.

Lio smiled a smile that did not reach his eyes. For now he would allow the youth to think he had been successful in his deceit. Lio had plotted a course to a nearby planet that would be a perfect facility for some mind probing. Its scientific exploration center was well known across the universe.

The intercom close to Lio buzzed. Lio leaned in to answer. His eyes remained locked with Hamen's as he spoke. "Lio here!"

"General, there is a craft approaching. It meets the specs of the vessel we listed on Jamaica 2."

"Indeed," Lio drawled. "It seems we are having a visitor. How many life sign aboard the vessel?"

"Just one; human," the voice replied.

"Extend our guest the beam of welcome." Lio laughed at his own humor before turning back to Hamen. "I will return to Trinz, but first it seems I have a guest to prepare for."

Lio ignored the guttural growl that emanated from the cell. He turned on his heel and proceeded towards the landing deck. He knew his tractor beam would bring Jenni straight to him, and he hoped he could appeal to her loyalty to find out more about the Trinz. Jenni's parents had been most obliging and were numbered among his best militia throughout his time as general. Lio recalled an application for navigation officer on his latest ship due to explore the Yankee Zone. He was sure he could arrange that position in exchange for some vital information on his prisoner. All in all, Lio was feeling quite confident about his bargaining position.

~ * ~

At the controls of the small ship, Jenni was too busy to think much about her plan. She was flying a craft meant for duel pilots, and her hands were skimming across the interactive screens in a frenzy of activity. It was as she was engaging the warp thrusters she felt the jolt. It was as if the ship had made contact with another vessel even though none were in the vicinity. Jenni froze as the controls ceased to respond to her touch. The ship was being dragged through space, and there was nothing she could do to prevent it.

Thinking fast, she pulled her hands from the screens and slipped from her seat. The ship maintained its course despite Jenni's absence from the controls. She looked around for a place to conceal herself. She thought if she had the element of surprise on her arrival, she may be able to break free and seek out Hamen. Jenni had no doubt General Lio was behind her abduction from space. She knew and had used the very same beams to pull obstacles from her path on board Chicago 3. Finding a loose panel at the rear of the vessel, Jenni climbed in and crouched down, pulling the panel into place behind her. She could no longer see her location but knew exactly where she was heading.

As the ship came to a standstill, Jenni surmised she was aboard the larger vessel. When the doors burst open, Jenni waited until they were all crammed inside the small vessel then jumped down lightly behind them. Pushing the door release button, she skipped through the closing doors and flashed a grin at the stunned faces of the trapped crew. Jenni ran as fast as she could, thinking on her feet as she made it across the open space of the landing bay. She ducked into an open doorway and paused, breathing heavily from the exertion.

Think, Jenni, she screwed her eyes up as she thought hard.

"Panel," she hissed.

Around the ship, information panels provided regular updates and onboard systems. Jenni scanned the empty corridor for a control station. She needed to move fast as backup would soon be summoned. It was a fifty-fifty decision, so Jenni chose to go right. She ran along in a straight line then followed the bends until she spotted what she was looking for at a junction in the passageways. As fast as she could, Jenni laid her finger on the panel. It recognized her as an employee and allowed her access. Jenni scanned the life signs aboard the ship. Tiny yellow dots represented the human occupants and various groups of colors displayed the other species on board. A lone blue dot at the rear of the vessel alerted Jenni to the presence of Hamen. She deduced he would be the only Trinz on board. Next, Jenni scanned for a map and visualized her route to the cells. Being a navigational engineer was a definite advantage when plotting a course.

Jenni traversed the corridors until she came to a secure door. This heralded the entrance to the cells. Jenni tried to use her fingerprint as she had earlier. When that failed, she tried to use her own access code on the flat screen panel but a red "No Entry" sign flashed across the display. Jenni growled in frustration. A single door stood between her and the man she wanted to reunite with; the man she needed to reunite with. In the short time they had spent together, an intense bond had formed. It was almost painful to be apart from him, and Jenni ached to be back in his company.

A though struck Jenni; a game she had played with her father when she was a little girl. She had a memory for numbers and her father had taught her his own access code among many other strings of numbers. It was the party-piece he delighted in showing to visitors who came to their home. Desperation brought the string of numerals to the fore of Jenni's mind. She punched in the code and squinted as if bracing for the red screen. Instead, a green entry sign filled the area. The door swung open, and Jenni was greeted by rows of cells. Not a soul could be seen and Jenni frowned at the lack of security.

"Hamen," she whispered.

"Jenni?" came the reply.

"It's me," Jenni smiled at the sound of his voice so close by.

"It's a trap! Run!" Hamen called out just as General Lio stepped out of the cell and faced her.

Chapter Thirteen

Loathing filled Jenni as she looked upon the beast responsible for the death of her parents and now the kidnap of Hamen. She looked at his tall, thin form with a crop of pure white hair combed down in a slick across his head. Cruel blue eyes regarded her with contempt and a hint of victory.

"Jenni Gravin, we meet at last," he said with a mocking tone.

"General Lio, I wish I could say it is my pleasure," Jenni bit out.

"I do not expect us to be friends," he said, "but we may be able to help one another."

"I'm listening," Jenni said flatly.

"I want to find Trinz. Your boyfriend, in there, claims not to know the way, so I need a navigator with a vested interest."

"What makes you think I know the way?" Jenni asked.

"I imagine he will dig a little deeper if I have you as bait," General Lio explained. "He may be more agreeable to my brain exploration to extract the information."

"No!" Jenni cried.

"Oh yes, my dear. You seem to forget I hold all the cards."

"I want to see him," Jenni held eye contact with the formidable general.

"Very well." General Lio stepped aside and gestured into the cell he had just vacated.

Jenni trotted forward and stood at the entrance to the cramped space. Hamen lay on the narrow cot, bound, with a vicious looking guard looming over him. His eyes locked onto hers brimming with regret.

"It's okay," she soothed. "We will work something out. I promise."

"So sweet," Lio mocked. "Now tell me how you two met?"

Hamen tried to shake his head, but Jenni had no intention of sharing anything with the warmonger before her.

"I forget," she lied smoothly.

"And how did he come to be aboard Chicago 3?" Lio probed. "There is no record of any Trinz arriving on any vessel. Records are quite thorough, so I am sure I would not have missed it."

"Haven't you destroyed enough of the universe without targeting another innocent race?" Jenni fumed. "Leave the Trinz alone. They ask for just one small piece of space. You have the rest of it."

"But I want it all," Lio smiled, revealing a row of crooked teeth. "I want to own the whole universe. I want to reach its end and know I have conquered all of it."

"You make me sick!" Jenni spat.

Lio raised his hand and struck her firmly across her cheek. The force sent Jenni off balance, and she fell against the smooth wall of the cell.

Hamen struggled against his bonds, crying out with a savage roar.

"Gag him," Lio commanded.

The guard complied and Lio looked between the pair of them with a cool contempt.

"I will have what I want from you both or you will be of no use to me. Things that are of no use to me are easily disposed of. I met a general recently who was no longer useful to me. Goaf, I think he was called. He is no longer a part of this universe. I will leave you two here to discuss your compliance."

With that General Lio and his guards left the cell and reactivated the force field. Jenni was left to loosen the bonds that held Hamen. She kissed his skin where the bonds had chaffed, lifting his reddened flesh to her lips with a gentle touch.

"Sorry," he said as he pulled her into his arms.

"Me too," Jenni said. "I had the perfect rescue planned."

Hamen laughed. The sound filled the small space and broke the tension. Encircled in each other's arms Jenni and Hamen stood still. Jenni rested her cheek against his chest. It felt good to hold him and gave her strength.

As Jenni stood safe in Hamen's warm embrace, a feeling of exhaustion washed over her. Her knees buckled and she slumped against Hamen. Without his bulky frame supporting her, she would have collapsed in a heap on the floor. Hamen led her to the tiny cot and sat her down. He lifted her legs and swung them onto the bed, allowing her weary body to lie down.

"Rest," he instructed. "You will need your strength for whatever Lio has in his twisted mind."

"Rest with me," Jenni murmured as her eyelids, heavy with fatigue, slowly closed.

Hamen perched himself on the edge of the narrow bed and cradled Jenni against him. She snuggled into his chest with a purr of satisfaction.

Hamen groaned as he stroked her back rhythmically. Jenni could fight the urge to sleep no longer and she slipped into welcome oblivion.

~ * ~

Cal had been fuming since Wren visited him a few days ago. He had been seated at his desk when a loud knock drew his attention. He knew Wren had arrived, his doorman always alerted him to any visitors. He also knew Wren had a female companion with him. Cal assumed Wren had found a new recruit for his chambers. Wren often brought girls that had taken his fancy and who would not be missed by any family. As a member of the Elder Panel, Wren had access to records he used to procure girls that fulfilled his own personal fantasies. Cal had no reason to believe this visit would be any different. That was until the door opened and Cal had come to face to face with the reason he resided as a prisoner on Trinz.

"You!" he said, glad of the fact he was sitting down as his legs felt decidedly weak.

"Hello, Cal," the woman said.

Even the sound of her voice stirred him. Cal recalled the nights spent with her, tasting the passion he had never again found. He remembered her voice crying out his name as she clung to him. The silence grew as the two faced each other.

Wren cleared his throat. "I believe you know Rein," he said.

"It has been a long time," Cal said at last.

"I had no idea you were here," Rein rushed to explain. "It was not until recently that I knew you had traveled here."

"Is that true?" Cal felt his anger surfacing as he turned to Wren.

"It was for the best," Wren shrugged in a noncommittal way.

"So, why now?" Cal voiced the obvious question.

His mind was racing as he tried to ignore the physical effect Rein's presence was having on him. Despite the bevy of women who worked with him, Cal had never been with another Trinz. His desire for vengeance far outweighed any desire he had and his loathing of the entire species made him impotent. Cal felt life stirring in his trousers and a pool of desire building in him. He looked over to Rein who was looking back at him in a daze. Her tongue traced the line of her lips as if she too recalled their time together.

"My son is lost," Rein beseeched him with her dark eyes. "He, too, passed through the Killanti Project and now is facing danger at the hands of General Lio. Lio seeks Trinz. His lust for power drives and possesses him. I want my son safe from him. I want my son back."

"He is the one who is lost?" Cal asked then added suspiciously, "Why come to me?"

"Hamen is...erm...well he is your son too," Wren admitted. "We need you to try and reach him."

"My what?" Cal bellowed. "You dare to come in here and announce that I am a father!"

"He is our son," Rein approached the desk and reached for Cal's hand.

Her very touch sent sparks dancing through Cal's body.

"Please," she appealed to him. "Help him."

Cal drew back his hand and dropped his head into his palms. He remained there for a full minute before he croaked, "What do you want me to do?"

~ * ~

In the pod, Cal looked up at the white metal that surrounded him. He was linked up with wires on his head and attached to his chest and arms. Part of him longed to see the lush green world of Killanti, but he knew he would be loath to return to his underground world afterwards. The drug injected into him was making him drowsy. His mind was wandering back to the lazy, passionate dreams he had once enjoyed. The smell of the chestnut hair lingered on the peripheral of his senses as the sterile pod morphed into the verdant fields of Killanti. Cal found himself beside a deep luminous pool. The water shimmered as its transparent surface rippled in the breeze. Cal inhaled deeply. His lungs filled with the clean air.

Cal considered the last twenty four hours of his life. Since learning he had fathered a son, he had been schooled intensely in the procedures of the Killanti Project. Wren and Ju had tutored him in what to say to Jenni and how to connect with her mind in the vortex of space. They taught him how to recognize her soul among the many he would encounter in his journey across space. Cal had sensed the animosity in Ju. His manner had been professional yet Cal had seen him bristle with inner tension. Already touched by the Trinz, Jenni would be easily drawn into the type of slumber that would transport her to Killanti. Her mind had been connected to the Project, and as Hamen's DNA substitute, Cal could pull her back into the Project. Rein informed him that she had not been a suitable match. It had been devastating to her that she could not help and it had pained the Panel to reveal to her the presence of Cal. Cal had been kept from her after the initial meeting, but he intended to seek her out when he had completed his mission. In fact, the thought of their next encounter was all that was keeping him going.

A slight sound interrupted Cal's musings. He turned as a beautiful girl appeared before him.

~ * ~

The scene cleared as Jenni realized she was back in the clearing by the pool where she first met Hamen. A figure stood by the azure pool with his eyes fixed firmly on her. Jenni walked slowly over. The breeze that felt so familiar caressed her face and carried the lush smell of the rich fauna.

"Jenni, I am Cal. I am Hamen's father. You must let him go. He is in grave danger and so is the planet he loves. If Lio reaches Trinz or Killanti, the universe will not survive."

"I have no hold on him," Jenni protested. "He is free to go. How can he leave? He is imprisoned on Lio's vessel."

"We know this. I have come to bring him home."

"How?" Jenni asked.

"You must release him. He is bound to you. We know not how or why but your bond has stretched through the universe and defied the laws of physical matter. You must break the tie by breaking his heart."

"No!" Jenni protested. "I cannot. I love him."

"If you love him, you must free him. He will be used as a tool for war. Lio will infiltrate his mind and track his memories to Trinz. Lio will then seek to conquer what is left of the universe. This cannot happen. The Trinz would rather kill Hamen than allow Lio access to their Killanti Project. I have convinced the Elder panel to reach out to you first," Cal explained gravely.

"I will do it," Jenni said, defeated by his words.

"It is the right choice," Cal assured her.

Jenni nodded sadly. She knew her time with Hamen would eventually need to end, but she was getting used to having him around. Her own heart lurched at the thought of what she had to do. Tears welled up in her eyes and her shoulders shook with grief.

"Jenni," a voice broke through her despair.

Jenni opened her eyes to see Hamen's concerned face inches from her own.

"Wake up, you are crying. What has upset you?"

Jenni averted her gaze from the love she saw in Hamen's eyes. She couldn't bear to hurt him, yet she was afraid for his safety if she did not.

"I can't do this anymore," she confessed. "I am going to talk to Lio. It is over, Hamen. I want to go home."

"Home?" Hamen echoed. "I thought home was where we both were." His face looked crushed as the implications of her cruel words hit him.

"Well, you thought wrong!" Jenni snapped waspishly. "I became stuck with you, but now I choose to leave. What we have is over."

"I see," Hamen's voice was only just audible. "I thought it was something more. I see I was mistaken."

Jenni said nothing. She fixed her eyes on a spot on the ceiling and stared up at it.

"Jen..." Hamen's voice faded.

Jenni turned to see his body translucent in the cell. As she watched in horror, his form faded and was gone.

"Stop!" the voice of General Lio thundering as he ran into the cell, washed over Jenni. All around her, the sounds distorted as blackness engulfed her.

~ * ~

Cal sat up and rubbed his temples. The machine seemed to push into his very skull and it ached.

"Well?" Wren's bearded face peered out from behind the monitor.

"I did what I could do," he snapped. "It is up to the girl now."

"Then let us hope you did enough," Wren added matter-of-fact.

"If you had been honest with me, this may have been avoided." Cal snapped.

Cal's eyes widened as the outline of a figure emerged in the room. It was hunched over and seemed to shimmer as if struggling to materialize. With a feral cry of despair, the shape became solid as two eyes regarded Cal.

Chapter Fourteen

Sitting in the navigation seat, Jenni gazed unseeing into the darkness of space. She lifted her arm and twirled the heavy tracking device locked in place around her wrist. General Lio had placed her on duty each day, and at night she was observed by a team of insomnia scientists. Straight after Hamen's disappearance, Jenni had been given a truth serum; a remnant of the early days of invasion. Lio told her that he used it to find out information about new planets. It saved him time and ensured him total victory. Lio had been fascinated by Jenni's confession.

The idea of access to a world gained in sleep intrigued him. The device attached to Jenni transmitted data about her reactions both physical and emotional. Lio would know if she made any sort of contact with Hamen, and he would manipulate her to draw out the coordinates to Trinz. Jenni seethed at her own betrayal. She knew Hamen would not come to her now after she had been forced to deny him. It was evident to her that the connection was based on the strength of their mutual attraction. Her parents' love had convinced Jenni that everyone had a soul mate, and she felt Hamen had been hers. Letting herself dwell on it brought fresh tears to Jenni's already swollen eyes.

Sleep was eluding her as she dreaded the depth of her betrayal in her dreams. Lio watched her like a cunning eyed hawk as she moved about in a daze from one task to another. His gaze seemed to be willing her to fall asleep and reveal the secrets he craved. Jenni refused to succumb to his demands and fought to keep her body from its inevitable betrayal.

As she sat at her screen, fulfilling her goal of manning a discovery vessel, the achievement seemed hollow. A dream job paled into insignificance after the love she shared with Hamen. Instead, Jenni plotted her escape. She thought of the small vessel that sat in the docking bay, abandoned yet temptingly available for an attempt at freedom. Her mind raced as she thought of a way she could reach the bay without raising the suspicions of Lio and his guard.

In the end, the answer came through an unlikely source. Jenni was sitting in the stark, sterile sleeping quarters that had become her home. Wired to machines, her sleep was closely monitored, resulting in an uncomfortable and restless slumber. She sat bolt upright, determined to prevent the disloyalty of her subconscious from being revealed. Jenni had no way of knowing if Hamen sought her out in his dreams. She hoped he would but knew his life and his world would be in mortal danger if he did.

"Pssst!" came a low voice from outside the chamber. "Jenni, are you in there?"

"Who is that?" Jenni asked, her suspicions aroused. Lately, she trusted no one and it seemed to be the best way to survive.

"I am a friend," the husky voice continued. Its low timbre told Jenni that it was male, probably of latter years. "I am a friend of Killanti. I have been sought to find you and bring you home."

"Home?" Jenni's voice was tinged with regret. "I had one once."

"You will have one again. You are being called to Killanti. Voices seek you across the universe. Do not turn your back on Killanti."

"How can I do anything? I am stuck here with wires watching my every thought." Jenni growled in frustration.

"You are not the only one to be reached through your dreams. I too have been selected. I hope to leave very soon. Be ready, I will take you with me."

"Who are you? Where can I find you?"

Even as she spoke, Jenni sensed the owner of the voice had vacated the space outside her cell. Her heart sank as despair once again replaced the glimmer of hope that had started to swell within her. As Jenni gave herself up to the overwhelming force of sleep, her eyes grew heavy and her head dropped forward as sleep won the inner war.

~ * ~

Hamen brooded as he looked out over the striking scene of the city before him. The weeks since his parting from Jenni had been among the hardest of his life. His emotions swung from rage to pain as he replayed her cruel words of rejection. He now faced the Elder Panel for the second time in his life as they repeated the tedious questions over and over again.

"I have told you all I know," Hamen snapped. "I woke up there, in her bed, and I tried to make my way back here. General Lio intercepted me then I returned here. It is that simple."

Hamen was reluctant to betray Timon's location so he had omitted him from his recount.

Ju asked, "What is this human to you? I see the boy I know and love before me, yet he seems so unlike the boy who left. What has changed son?"

Hamen looked at his father. His eyes filled with pity. "I know love," he explained. "Physical love. I loved Jenni with my body. We are as one."

"No!" Ju exploded. "What of the risk? The risk is to your health and the health of the planet. Once before we loved as you describe but disease almost brought us to the brink of extinction. Sexual love is the past. We have evolved."

"We are missing out on so much!" Hamen could not keep his opinion quiet any longer. "It is the most glorious feeling! When can I leave to seek out Jenni?"

"The girl does not want you," Wren interrupted. "She sent you back here. It is over, son."

"I am not your son!" Hamen retaliated. "I am the son of a human, a fact you all forgot to tell me."

"It was for the best," Wren explained. "For the Project. We could not risk the Project."

"Damn the Project!" Hamen exploded.

He turned and stormed from the room, straight past his mother who tried to restrain him with a gentle hand on his arm.

"Not now!" he blazed, instantly regretting his outburst as a hurt look crossed her face. "I'll speak to you later," he added, gently taking her hand from his arm and tucking it back into her own body.

Slightly calmer, Hamen strode from the room. He was restless and did not know where he was going. He walked around the streets until he found himself outside the door Wren had taken him to once before. He raised his hand to knock when the door opened.

"He said you'd come," the burly doorman winked jovially.

"Who said I'd come? Wren?" Hamen was confused. He hadn't even known he was heading this way.

"Not Wren, that dirty old dog. The boss, Cal."

"Cal?" Hamen repeated. "He is here?"

"It's where he always is," sang the man cheerily. "Where else would he be? He's a prisoner, you know. Follow me, lad."

Hamen followed the man's wide shoulders down the same corridor adorned with pornographic images. He was blind to the scenes, and his only thought was how the massive man could fit along the narrow walkway without getting stuck. All too soon, they came to a paneled door. The doorman gave a brief knock then swung open the wooden door.

"Here 'e is," he called out, "just like you said."

"Thank you, Nat," Cal appeared at the door and clapped his hand on the bigger man's shoulders.

Hamen felt uncomfortable now. He didn't know what had brought him here, but seeing Cal was the last thing he expected.

"Come on in," Cal said. "It is nice to see you."

"What...I mean why?"

"I live here," Cal began to fill in the blanks. "It is my prison. I am here at the insistence of the Elder Panel, so I thought I would make the best of it. I decided to test the theory that all desire had been bred out of this cold-hearted race."

"You are my father?" Hamen knew he was stating the obvious but could not help himself.

"I think there is a resemblance, don't you?" Cal asked.

"I need to go back," Hamen got to the point. "Jenni is still there with Lio. He has her."

"You can't go back," Cal said. "She does not want you. The connection is lost."

"No!" Hamen denied the charge. "The connection is there. She loves me. Lio must have wiped her memory or something. I must get back before they wipe mine and I forget her."

Cal looked at the desperation in the eyes of his son. He knew that look. He knew the love that filled his son. He knew it because he had felt it too.

"I loved your mother," he said. "We came together in our dreams

104

then I found myself here. She was nowhere to be seen. I thought she had abandoned me. I thought it for twenty five years, but she never knew. They never told her."

Cal's mouth twisted in rage as the familiar feelings rose up in him. He could not stand to see his son become as bitter as he was.

"I went to her," he spoke quietly.

"Went to whom?" Hamen frowned at the confession.

"Jenni. They sent me to tell her to let you go. They feared for Killanti. I feared for you."

"What?" Hamen yelled, enraged by what he was hearing.

"I told her to let you go. If she loved you, I said. If she loved you, she must make you believe that she didn't so you could travel back to safety."

Cal looked at the light of hope returning to his son's eyes. "I'm sorry," he added.

"You mean she still loves me?" Hamen said, the corners of his mouth turned up as a twinkle reached his eye. It was soon replaced by a frown. "She is out there with him, alone."

"'Bout time I left this rock," Cal said with a matching twinkle in his own eyes. "What say we call in a few favors, son?"

"What are we waiting for?" Hamen replied as father and son made their way out from the shadows and into the light of a bright Trinz day.

Chapter Fifteen

A dark presence lingered in Jenni's peripheral vision. She knew she was back in Killanti, but this was a darker more eerie place that she found herself looking at. The darker canopy overhead stifled the light and cast menacing shadows over the grass below. Jenni was frustrated that her dream had brought her here. She tried to control her mind enough to allow her to sleep without the dreams; without passing into the realm of Killanti.

"Jenni, you have been away too long," a low, scratchy voice rasped close to her yet the figure was masked by the dense undergrowth.

"Who's there?" Jenni asked, her voice cracked as she spoke, fear gripping her heart.. She sensed hostility in the atmosphere but the presence remained aloof. "Show yourself!" she demanded, trying to sound braver than she felt.

A low chuckle resonated in the enclosed space. "I do not think you are in a position to make demands. I am here to ensure the safety of my people. You, a mere human, have posed a threat more serious than anything the Trinz have faced for millennia."

"M...m...e?" stuttered Jenni. "I have done nothing but dream a dream forced upon me from a race that considers itself better than the rest of the universe." Rage was beginning to replace fear as Jenni began to realize her predicament. She had been manipulated from the start, first by Hamen then Lio then by the man who demanded she give up Hamen and return him to Trinz. "I have done nothing but dance to your tune, and I will not play your game any longer."

"Temper, temper" the voice mocked. "I see the spark that ignited Hamen to lust for you. He certainly was not so keen when I tried to introduce him to the ways of the flesh."

Jenni gasped. She knew there was some corruption on Trinz. Hamen had hinted as much to her, but what was it to do with her and what did this mysterious figure want with her? More than that, how had he been able to find her?

"Mind working overtime, is it? I can almost hear your brain processing the information," the rasping voice continued to taunt her. "Allow me to put you out of your misery. I am Wren, head of the Elder Panel which is responsible for the Killanti Project. I serve as mentor and guardian to the Communers. I have also become involved in the, well let's just call it the underworld of the Trinz society. I am keen to explore the old ways, the ways that focused on the pleasures the flesh can offer. I find you would make an interesting diversion for some of the better paying customers. A human girl would be quite an interesting addition to our rooms."

Jenni baulked. She would have to think fast or she could find herself prisoner of another unscrupulous man who was out for his own gain. Jenni had seen enough old movies clips to know if the bad guy revealed his plan to you, there was not much hope of an escape. She willed her mind to retrace itself back to the ship where she may be a prisoner of Lio, but at least she had the hope of an escape from the ally she had heard outside the door.

"I just need you to see me," the voice of Wren continued. "I am lingering at the edge of your vision. I need you to perceive me, to make the final connection. Hear me, Jenni, and see me in your mind."

Jenni smiled in triumph. *He can't get to me! He is stuck observing me and trying for the connection.* Jenni surmised Hamen had made the link to her with his desire to rescue her from the pool. This time, there was no danger and she would ensure there would be none. Jenni froze and forced her eyes shut. She stood motionless, grinning in satisfaction as an audible hiss reached her ear.

Jenni did not know just how long she stood there, her mind focusing on blocking out the pleas of Wren. He sneered and coaxed then begged and demanded but Jenni remained resolute.

"He's here you know," Wren finally revealed in a snide whisper. "Hamen is here on Trinz. Come with me and you can see him again."

Jenni inhaled deeply. She held her breath in as her mind raced. Infinite possibilities bombarded her head, but the instinctive dislike of Wren prevailed. Jenni remained staunchly still and closed herself off from the emotions that flooded her. She would have liked nothing more than to give herself over to the possibility, however slight, that she could be reunited with Hamen. Thoughts of her conversation with Cal still haunted her. The last thing she wanted was to put him in danger even if it meant never seeing him again. Jenni ached with pain as that thought entered her head. She had to believe a force greater than both of them would eventually bring them back together.

"Gone?" the voice, stronger now and more commanding. "What do you mean he's gone? Cal too? I am on my way?"

Jenni sensed the absence at once. She frowned as she made sense of what she had heard.

It must be him. He is coming for me.

A slow smile spread over Jenni's face as the verdant world around her began to disappear.

The smile was still fixed to her face as she opened her eyes back in the tiny cell. Every pore in her body sang. It was as if she were anticipating the most exciting event of her life. It took a split second for Jenni to recall why her body felt so alive.

"He's coming back," she said as her memory returned.

"I never doubted it," General Lio's voice came from the entrance to the cell. "I sensed there was something between you that he would want more of. Maybe I was too hasty in dismissing you. You may have more to offer than your navigational skills."

A small trickle of saliva ran down Lio's chin as he leaned forward and leered at Jenni. His eyes roved over her, taking in all of her curves and lingering on her breasts.

Jenni stood up and pulled herself to her full height.

"Take your filthy eyes off me!" she demanded. "I am here against my will, but I will kill you if you lay as much as a hand on me."

Lio's expression changed to one of revulsion. "Some may appreciate the fire of high spirits," he spat, "I prefer a more placid mate."

Jenni sighed as she moved past him. "I have a shift to get to," she said before walking briskly towards the navigation area.

When she felt it was safe to pause, Jenni stopped and leaned forward. She rested her hands on her knees and took in great gulps of air. Her mind raced as she considered what had happened in the last few hours. Hamen had gone; now he was on his way back; Lio was a bigger threat than she had first given him credit for and a mysterious friend was trying to help her escape from this prison she had found herself in. It was all so bizarre yet was her reality at this moment in time and she had to deal with it.

Jenni breathed slowly in through her nose and out through her mouth. Her breath that had been coming in shuddering gulps began to calm down and become more rhythmic. Jenni took stock of her current situation.

"First things first," she said to the empty corridor.

As she stood erect to proceed to her shift, a man emerged from a doorway close by. He was around fifty and had salt and pepper hair with a long angular nose. He was tall and thin but with the appearance of strength. Jenni smiled a polite greeting, imagining he would pass by on his way to wherever he was headed. Instead, he stopped close to her and looked intensely into her eyes.

"The time is almost upon us," he said quickly.

Jenni started as she recognized the voice that had infiltrated her cell the night before.

"We must make haste in our departure. Tomorrow could be too late," he continued with urgency.

Jenni hesitated. She wondered how much to confess to this stranger. His darting eyes seemed to hold no guile and Jenni was weary of feeling alone. Despite these fleeting thoughts, she decided to err on the side of caution and keep her own secrets.

"What do you suggest?" Jenni asked instead.

The man seemed to hesitate as if he sensed her reticence. Finally, he replied.

"I will meet you on the observation deck after your shift. From there we can slip into the maintenance routes and make our way to the shuttle bay. Lio always has a shuttle prepped and ready for takeoff, and I have a contact in the security office. He, too, has been dreaming of a certain place."

Again the man's eyes darted from side to side as if he expected to see an eavesdropper in the vicinity.

"What makes you think I will come?" Jenni asked matter-of-fact.

The man looked surprised as if he had never considered the possibility of her not attending the rendezvous. He frowned then shrugged. "I am going whether you come or not so you must decide for yourself. This is not a rescue, merely the offer of a lift."

His tone reassured Jenni. She smiled abashed by her mistrust. "I will be there," she said decisively.

As soon as the words had been spoken, Jenni felt as if a weight had been lifted from her shoulders. The man flashed her one last tight smile then sauntered off in the direction he had been originally headed.

Jenni's step felt like it had a spring in it as she proceeded to her post in the navigation area. Her thoughts turned to Hamen and his broad chest. She longed to rest her cheek against it and bask in the glory of his muscled form. Just the thought of the path her hands would trace made Jenni ache deep inside herself and she tried in vain to dismiss her carnal desires. Her mind was filled with images of their love making. His hands on her, his length buried deep inside her and his eyes filled with lust as his gaze locked with hers as they reached the peak of their desire as one. Jenni shuddered as if her climax had been real. Her upper thighs ached with longing for his presence between them. Tears pooled in her eyes as she recalled the look of hurt that seemed to linger in the room as he slowly vanished. Jenni was unsure how Hamen would receive her, but she knew with the courage of her convictions she had to find him and try to right the wrong.

~ * ~

Hamen was having erotic thoughts of his own. As the small vessel blazed a trail through the universe, his mind wandered to the reunion he could expect with Jenni. He knew she had acted from love and the thought of it filled his heart with joy. His one desire was to find her and reassure her that he knew why she had sent him away. Hamen allowed his thoughts to linger on what he would do after he had seen the look of acceptance in her eyes. He imagined his big hands encircling her waist as her body molded into his, mirroring his shape and pressing hungrily against him. Hamen felt his manhood throb as his vision morphed into an image of Jenni wildly riding him. Her breasts were bouncing tantalizingly before his dry mouth. Her hair fell in waves over her shoulders, moving over her face as she swayed and gyrated welcoming him deeper into her. To Hamen the image felt so real he could smell the musky scent of her arousal and taste the salty sweat of her skin on the air. The fact her hair was partially obscuring her face sent Hamen into a frenzy of desire. The mystery of a anonymous figure yet one he knew by instinct was a heady combination.

"You seem distracted," Cal observed wryly as he turned his head to look at his son closely. "I have seen enough of nature to know a fantasy when I see one. She must be very special this Jenni."

"She is," Hamen said simply.

He forced his mind back to his reality which was a cramped cockpit on a small shuttle ship heading towards the Victor Zone. Their plan was to make it to Jamaica 2 to enlist the help of Timon in their quest for Lio's militia ship. Hamen had been all for giving chase to the larger vessel, but Cal had managed to convince his hot headed son to adopt a more sensible plan.

"Think with your head, not your balls," he had reprimanded his offspring. "There will be time for the latter when we find her."

Hamen had been reluctant to deviate so far from the trail but saw the wisdom of the older man's plan after several heated debates. Cal had set the course dictated to him by Hamen, and now the craft was heading to enlist the help of Timon. Hamen hoped the big Trinz had recovered from the knock to the head General Lio had inflicted on him. Not for a second did Hamen consider his friend had been mortally injured. Hamen knew him to be resilient and fully intended to find him in fine health, probably enjoying the delights of his beautiful companion once again.

Hamen's main concern was for Jenni. He feared for her safety aboard Lio's ship since his departure. He knew she would be of little use to Lio without him and knew what type of man Lio was. The sooner Hamen could persuade Timon to help him the happier he would feel.

Hamen practically cried with relief when the deep tones of Timon reverberated through the small vessel.

"That better be you, Hamen!" he boomed. "One Trinz a year is enough for me to handle. Hello to you too, Jenni."

"May I introduce you to Cal, my father," Hamen replied. "Jenni is not the human life form you detected. She is a guest of Lio and I want your help to rescue her."

"Straight to the point!" Timon laughed out loud, startling the pair in the ship. "Come on down and we'll draw up a battle plan. Welcome to Jamaica 2, Cal."

~ * ~

Jenni's shift seemed to drag on forever. She watched as the endless blackness of space stretched out before her. The tiny points of light that heralded their destination remained elusively distant. Jenni was reminded of a story she had heard as a child where a wonderful place existed past the second star to the right. Jenni half hoped Trinz and Killanti were not there as Lio would not rest until he had found it. Another part of her held onto the hope it was just were Hamen was waiting for her to come to him.

"Time's up!" one of the other navigation officers bent low to her ear. "Looks like you've been off for hours though. Somewhere better than this, I hope."

"I hope so too," Jenni mused.

She rose from the large seat and collected her personal tray.

Emptying the contents into her hand, Jenni refastened the silver necklace that had hung around her neck since she was sixteen. Its round disc portrayed St. Christopher, the patron saint of travel, and Jenni had worn it religiously ever since.

Jenni paused at the door. Right would take her back to the cell where Lio would track her dreams whilst left would take her to the strange man who had offered her an escape and a chance to seek Hamen. Choosing left, Jenni lengthened her stride and was soon standing at the edge of the busy observation deck. She spotted the man at once. He had the air of one who was trying too hard to blend into the crowd. Jenni approached him with a wary smile.

"Jenni," she extended her hand.

"Mitts," he replied then added, "Don't ask. It's short for Mitchell."

"I am ready, Mitts," Jenni said.

"Follow me," he said as he turned towards a service door and disappeared inside.

A maze of tunnels greeted them. Jenni looked bemused as she turned her head from left to right. Mitts seemed more confident. With a quick glance over his shoulder to make sure she was following, he set off this way and that down the labyrinth of access passageways. Lined with wires and humming with the demand for power, the corridors echoed with a macabre tune. Jenni had to jog to keep pace with the long, athletic strides of her companion. Her senses were ablaze with thoughts of escape and adrenalin ran through her veins with each step she took she was closer to her liberty.

~ * ~

In a larger ship equipped for battle, Timon sat behind Hamen as he deftly guided it into deep space. Five burly Jamaicans sat, strapped into

114

their own seats, grim faces set into determined expressions of revenge. They had not forgotten their incarceration at the hands of Lio and jumped at the chance to join a small band bent on outsmarting him. The men were loyal to Timon and would have followed him anywhere. Hamen had been thankful for the decisive way Timon rallied the men and said his goodbyes to an emotional Hope before readying a ship for the journey. Cal and Timon hit it off at once and Timon enjoyed hearing the story of Cal's gradual corruption of the Trinz elite.

"Serves them right!" he bellowed, his voice ripe with mirth. "Oh! I wish I could see them come and go, their pants well and truly caught down around their ankles."

Cal laughed with him, although his face had taken on a slightly shamed appearance under the scrutiny of Hamen.

The ship passed through Zone after Zone, powered by a remnant of Trinz technology that Timon salvaged and added to the vessel. Debris flashed past. In recent times, less and less traffic congested space. The early Zones, still populated by most of the human race thrived with travel and exploration but deeper into the universe only occasional vessels with high capacity engines could make the long distances between planets.

Restlessly, Hamen punched out coordinates on the touch screen pad.

"Watch my ship!" Timon playfully punched Hamen's arm. "I have lent this to you on good faith."

He was rewarded with a low feral growl.

"Temper, temper!" Timon teased, his big face breaking into a playful grin.

"How far could they have traveled?" Hamen asked, refusing to be drawn into Timon's tormenting, even if it was harmless banter.

"Quite a way in one of the navigator ships. They are equipped with all the same technologies as the militia ships in case they encounter any resistance to their exploration. Which they often do," he added with a shrug.

"Lio would have the best of the fleet," Cal added. "I recall meeting him once when I was stationed in the Echo Zone. He struck me as the sort of man who would insist on nothing but the best. Even then he was relentlessly pursuing the Trinz. He heard whispers of incidences of the dream connection but could not find anyone to aid him in his quest. Those that finally departed by conventional means left no trace of their trail at all. Lio has been both fascinated and frustrated by it for many years now. Yet the Trinz remain one step ahead of him at all times."

"They had him watched," Timon said simply. "Many of those we contact have a role to play before they are called home to Killanti. I suppose it is a test of their loyalty and gives time for their Communer to implant the ideas into their dreams."

"How come Hamen and I were able to travel physically through the dream?" Cal asked. "I have sought the answer in vain for the last twenty five years of my incarceration. None seem able to explain."

"It is a good question indeed," Timon replied. "And I rather think that if the Trinz had the answer, they would be harnessing the connection to bring all by that means. It is certainly a safer option to maintain the secrecy of Killanti's location. Imagine if the Trinz could transport people telepathically. They would harvest the universe and build new worlds in the blink of an eye. Maybe it is for the best that only two have experienced the phenomenon. They are not the gods some consider themselves to be."

"I agree with you there," said Cal. "I have seen the seedier side of the Trinz and can confirm they are no better or worse than any race across the universe."

"I am beginning to see that for myself," Hamen concurred with a heavy heart.

It was certainly confronting to face the truth of your species. A rite of passage often came with the adult realization that many of the truths of childhood were not all as black and white as they once seemed to be.

Hamen turned his thought back to Jenni. It was never for very long that they left her, but Hamen still felt a twinge of shame when she left his head for a few seconds or minutes. Now that he knew she had not betrayed him, he could not believe how stupid he had been to think she would have. Her eyes looking up into his as they shared their passion now haunted his waking and sleeping. Hamen still dreamed of her, but his dreams lacked the physical presence of the one he craved. He longed to be reunited with her and spend however long it took to beg her forgiveness. Hamen felt the stirrings below his waist as he visualized her astonishment then delight at the shape of his tongue. He had been delighted at the way he could use it as a tool for her pleasure, surrounding her delicate nub with it then bringing the two sides together to bring her to the brink of satisfaction over and over again. Hamen could taste the creamy musk as he imagined her delicate thighs encircling his head and tightening around him to bring him closer to her sex. He shuddered and dragged his mind back to the task at hand.

"You must stop doing that," Timon groaned, clutching his own genitals in mock agony. "I shall soon be looking towards my Jamaican friends with lustful intentions if you do not stop wearing your arousal like a badge of honor."

Cal's laugh rocked through the small cabin whilst the Jamaican guys looked at Timon with horrified expressions.

"Do not worry, my friends," Timon boomed. "You are not my type. Too flat here!" His hands gestured across his chest making the shape of two mounds.

The Jamaicans laughed with evident relief and nodded, adding their own imaginary breasts and leering at one another.

"Great! Now you are all horny and I left my best girls behind on Trinz," Cal added to the banter.

Hamen looked at his father and smiled. He had known this man for such a short time yet found it hard to believe he had led the life he had over the past twenty five years. If he had been worthy of the Trinz's attention then he must have had some integrity.

"What made you do what you have done on Trinz?" Hamen asked after a while. "I don't really buy the whole revenge story."

"It is amazing what love can do to people," Cal explained. "Love can drive us to things we never thought we would be capable of. To answer your question, it is hard to explain for it has only been over the last few days traveling with you that I have really sat back and thought about the last twenty five years. Sometimes we just fall into circumstances that gradually take us away from who we thought we were and who we thought we would be. With Wren and his tastes, I suppose I just wanted to please my jailer in case it led me to a reunion with your mother. When I realized it never would, I suppose I became a bitter man full of hate. From there I evolved to numbness and denial. It seemed easier that way. I lost my fight. There was nothing to fight for until I found out about you. Now, I have the chance to right some of the wrongs and make a fresh start. We should all be allowed to do that, shouldn't we?"

Hamen nodded. He too was headed for a fresh start and hoped he would not be too late for it.

"I think I've picked up a trail," Timon interrupted. "Too big to be a run around and it has traces of the particles used in light speed synthesizing."

"This ship is amazing!" Hamen praised, noting the pride in Timon's face as he spoke.

"Amazing what twenty five years in exile can do for a man," he joked flippantly. "I will just lay in a course to track the particles then we can sit back and have some shut eye. The trace is faint so we have much space to make up. Looks like they're headed towards the Twins of Trinz."

Cal arched his eyebrows in a question.

"The duel stars that herald the start of the solar system that is home to Trinz and Killanti," Timon explained. "The planets orbit both suns, overlapping in their paths allowing the planets to be almost impossible to be mapped. It is one of the reasons their locations can remain such a secret. The planets are never in the same place long enough to be plotted and the duel paths create too many calculable combinations. It is a wonder actually that the planets don't collide more often."

"More often?" echoed Cal.

"Trinz folklore speaks of only once and the effects were so vast and catastrophic it is said to have sparked the creation of the rest of the universe. It is one of the reasons the Trinz feels so responsible for the rest of the universe. They think they created it."

Cal shook his head in wonder. "That's certainly not the way our species tell it," he said.

~ * ~

Jenni had lost her bearing totally. She had no idea the ship was so big, but she felt like she had been walking for hours. Mitts maintained his relentless pace and Jenni could feel her heart beating loudly against her chest. An occasional breath that verged upon a sob caught in her throat rewarding her with a scathing look from her companion.

"Shhhhh!" he snapped each time her body betrayed her in this way.

Suddenly and without warning just as Jenni was ready to give up and return to face the wrath of Lio, Mitts came to an abrupt halt in front of her. Jenni careened into him and bumped her head on his rigid back. He turned and gave her another of his withering looks.

"Sorry!" Jenni mumbled.

"Just ahead is the opening to a maintenance shaft," he explained quickly.

As he spoke, Mitts' eyes shifted as if he were expecting to be discovered at any minute. His actions made Jenni nervous, her senses moved to high alert as she too scanned the area for danger. Relieved none was evident, she turned her full attention back to the plan.

"One at a time we will crawl through the hatch and make our way to docking bay 13. Strange how that is Lio's lucky number, but it is where he keeps a vessel; more of an escape pod really, I suppose. He has it fueled and ready to take off at a moment's notice."

"They say rats will run from a sinking ship," Jenni joked.

"How does one so young know such an old Earth saying?" Mitts asked.

"My parents educated me well on Earth and all of its history," Jenni explained. "I probably know around ten thousand years of history up here." She tapped her head as she spoke.

"Come then," Mitts tone turned back to a businesslike one. "I would like very much to hear more from Earth when we are up and away."

"Jenni smiled, "And I would like to learn more of your dreams."

The escape went according to plan. Jenni felt a sense of déjà vu as she recalled her similar flight from Chicago 3; only that time she was with a man who she found hard to keep her hands off. She felt laughter bubble up inside her as she thought of his snarling noises when he thought her to be flirting. Jenni shivered as she thought of his possessiveness. It thrilled her to think he desired her so much he reacted in such a primal way.

On board the small vessel, Jenni allowed her hopes to surface. They had managed to walk through security thanks to another human who had been touched in his dreams by Killanti. Jenni was curious about the experiences others had. She knew her contact had been unique, but how had the Trinz convinced other humans to leave their lives and commit to a dream world that may not even exist. Jenni had grown up with tales of races that would lure unsuspecting humans to their deaths with promises of a new Earth. It was a well-known weakness of the human race that they yearned for a home world that equaled the one they destroyed. Enemies would take that weakness and use it to infiltrate and destroy their foe.

"If something seems too good to be true, it probably is." Jenni recalled her father's words of wisdom. Her eyes widened as she considered maybe she was now being lured to her doom.

Was Hamen really capable of such deception? Is Killanti really a new Eden or is it just a cover up for a slave world or worse?

Jenni wished, and not for the first time that day, Hamen was there to reassure her. He would set her troubled mind at rest and sooth her anxiety.

Jenni and Mitts were now headed towards the twin stars. Their pace was faster than the cumbersome ship they escaped from, but Jenni knew Lio would soon be in pursuit. Their trail would be easy to trace, and they were in grave danger of leading him straight to the place he desired to find the most.

"What is the plan now?" she asked Mitts, still keeping her voice low, from habit now not necessity.

"We need to ditch this vessel," his words concurred with her thinking. "And it may seem weird but I need to sleep. It is the only way I can connect with my Communer."

"What is your Communer called?" Jenni was fascinated by another being that had connected with a Trinz.

"We say no names," Mitts began with a frown on his face as if he were trying to remember the details of his encounter. "To be honest, I couldn't even tell you if they are a male or female. It is just a presence at the corner of my eye. It is like I know they are there, but I can't quite perceive them."

Jenni knew exactly what he meant. It had been like that for her too for so long.

"And you?" Mitts asked.

Jenni hesitated. She still did not know that this man was completely trustworthy and she held fast to her and Hamen's story, unwilling to share it details. "Ur... I...well we...we sort of met," she stammered. "I can't explain really. I just know he put himself in danger because of me, and I need to find him."

"It is on Killanti they want you, they want us both."

"Well, that will be a start," Jenni breezed. She was glad he hadn't pursued his questioning. Jenni sensed Mitts was happy not to know her details. As he had said before, it was a lift not a rescue. Jenni was sure that once on Killanti she could find a way to reach Hamen.

"The sensors have picked up a planet just outside the next galaxy," Mitts noted. "It seems to have a sustainable atmosphere. There are life signs there but not human; nothing recognized by this ship's technology either. Interesting."

"How is it maintaining an atmosphere so far from the galaxy?" Jenni's training was jumping to the fore. Her experience discovering new planets and races would be an asset.

"It seems to be in the gravitational pull of the duel suns," Mitts also sounded like he knew a thing or two about space. "An anomaly, I suppose."

Jenni wasn't so sure. In her experience there was a purpose for everything.

"Plotting a course," Mitts sang out cheerfully.

Jenni settled into her seat as the next stage of her destiny approached.

~ * ~

"It is not on any charts I have accessed," Hamen frowned at the tiny dot that had appeared on his screen. "I don't even see how it can be a planet. It is not inside a galaxy nor does it have an orbit path around either of the duel suns."

Timon and Cal brought up the image on their own screens. They both studied it for several minutes before speaking.

"It definitely is a planet. It even has a fully sustainable atmosphere," Timon voiced what Hamen had already observed.

"Life signs are present but not identified," Cal added. "A ship has passed this way recently too,"

Hamen frowned at that last piece of information. No ships should have been this far from the Zoned areas of the universe. Whoever it had been was getting dangerously close to the system that housed Trinz. Hamen now had another problem to solve. He would need to rid Trinz of the danger of discovery and that meant pursuing the ship down to the little anomaly sitting on his screen. He scowled in frustration as the universe seemed, once again, to be keeping him from the woman he loved.

"Set a course," he barked at his two startled companions.

Chapter Sixteen

The rattling sounds that seemed to be tearing the ship apart, told Jenni they had entered the atmosphere of the mysterious planet. She knew the flames would be licking the outside of the hull and she was thankful the vessel was sturdy. Mitts maintained control of the small ship expertly and used the coordinates supplied by the planet to navigate a landing. The landing area itself, when it finally came into view, gave them both a start. It appeared to be on the top of a tall building that stretched up into the sky above a layer of cloud. The planet itself was not visible through the pinky layer of clouds. A large geometric shape on top of the structure seemed to be the target area and a large light shone up to guide them. Jenni, surplus to the landing requirements, was free to observe as the landing dock got clearer.

The building was made of metal yet it appeared to be a patchwork of rusty pieces roughly welded together. Jenni was unsure it would even hold the weight of their vessel.

"It doesn't look very strong," Jenni voiced her concerns.

"Too late to turn back now!" Mitts said as he guided the ship to land perfectly on the unusual geometric design.

"Here goes then!" Jenni said as the door to the vessel hissed open.

A high pitched sound assaulted Jenni's ears at once. It was a shrill whistle that set her teeth on edge.

"What is that?" Jenni asked.

"Might be an altitude thing," Mitts explained. "I can't tell how high up we actually are."

The pair climbed out and stood on the deck that was indeed a patchwork of metal pieces. Jenni saw the door of a spacecraft as well as some panels that contained the names of ships in the mismatched quilt effect. There were both so intent on what lay beneath their feet they missed the approach of two uniformed officials.

Jenni studied the pair. They were a race she had never encountered before, but their appearance did not faze her. Living among a myriad of races her whole life made her accepting of all difference. This species were around half the height of an average human. Their quick red eyes were sizing up the intruders, but they seemed to mean no harm. The beings were clothed with a colored sash that seemed to indicate rank. Tufts of colorful hair stuck up on their heads between two pointed ears. Their noses twitched incessantly and two large teeth protruded from their tiny mouths. They rather reminded Jenni of a pet white mouse she once had as a child. She longed to peek behind them to see if a long tail grew.

A series of terrible squeaks emanated from the rodent-like beings causing Mitts and Jenni to cover their ears. The creatures stopped at once as one pulled something from his large trouser pocket.

Jenni marveled as pair of replica human ears were placed over her own. The soft downy feel of the simulated skin settled upon her own ears and attached behind. She turned to see Mitts with the same look of awe on his face. Suddenly, the sounds of the planet were audible to Jenni. She could hear the sounds of industry, metallic hammering sounds. A sort of music carried on the air which again had a very robotic melody.

"Welcome," one of the plant's inhabitants said. "We are Guardians of the system known as Para D.I.S. You have been selected to enter and will be directed to the planet Killanti. Please follow us."

Mitts nodded to Jenni as they watched the retreating backs of the two guardians. Jenni smiled to herself as she saw the proud swing of a fine tail protruding from the rear of the garments.

Two doors opened ahead and Jenni recognized the familiar setting of a lift. The guardians pressed a button, and Jenni felt her stomach lurch as if the floor had disappeared from under her.

"What happens next?" Jenni asked when her insides had recovered from the shock of falling.

"You will be put to sleep," the guardian who had done all the talking so far replied. "Then you will be contacted with directions. Only those with a connection to the Trinz can see us here at the edge of the galaxy," he explained.

Jenni paled as his words resonated. She would not be contacted. Her connection was broken. Would they let her leave?

Her thoughts were interrupted by the doors opening. A large room stretched out before them with an eclectic mix of chairs lining the walls. They all looked as if they had come from various space craft over the years. The range spanned generations of fashion and design.

"Where do you get all this stuff?" Jenni couldn't help but ask.

"Space junk," a new voice spoke as another creature approached them. "You would be surprised at what reaches us here. Everything ends up here eventually, and I do mean everything."

This guardian was evidently female. Her chest was dotted with engorged glands and her tufts of hair were longer and styled in a more feminine way."We are the buffer for the Para D.I.S. galaxy. Nothing is permitted to enter there without permission. We collect everything here and use what they do not require."

Jenni was sure the guardian added a leer in her direction as she spoke the last few words.

126

"And where is here?" Jenni asked. "Does this planet have a name?"

"We have many names. We are known to many races and each have a tale of us. The Trinz have named us Purr Gate."

"Para D.I.S. and now Purr Gate," Mitts scoffed. "What's next, the stairway to heaven?"

"Come," the female added. She looked decidedly un-amused at Mitts' attempt at humor.

Jenni, however, had paled at the connection. Mitts and Jenni were directed to a row of seats on the far side of the room. No sooner had they sat down than another female guardian appeared with a tray of drinks. The brew was slightly steaming and an unappealing green color.

"Drink and you will enter a sleep that will connect you to your Communer."

Mitts shrugged and downed his brew in one long gulp. Jenni paused then began to sip hers.

"Better if it's down in one!" slurred Mitts as he slumped into the seat and closed his eyes.

After one taste, Jenni decided he was right and forced the burning liquid down her throat. The sensation was instant. It reached her legs and made her glad she was sitting down. Her head spun and felt as if it were too heavy for her shoulders. Her eyelids were like lead and they closed in slow motion as the room disappeared from her view.

As she was drifting off, Jenni could hear voices all around her. She could not tell if it were a part of her dream or if it was the guardians in the room with her.

"Masters!" they chorused. "Masters are here!"

~ * ~

"Jenni! Jenni! Wake up! I need you to wake up!" Hamen's voice was urgent.

He had scarce been able to believe his eyes when he was shown to a room full of what looked like chairs from space vessels and seen a slumbering form in the corner of the room. The tousled blonde hair coupled with the physical jolt that slammed through Hamen's body was enough for him to know who sat, hunched up and sleeping there.

"Jenni?" he voiced his question out loud; a question he already knew the answer to.

"She has not yet made the vital connection with her Communer. Her companion has been sent on his way. His path was clear. This one may need to remain here with us."

Hamen did not like the look of the eager glint in the guardian's eye. He knew, as did most of the Trinz, what became of the races no longer worthy of Killanti. Natural wastage, it had always been seen as, but now, caught in the reality of a soul lost, Hamen felt a knot of disgust within him. The guardians were a scavenger race, brought to guard the entrance to the end of the universe. It was the place where both Trinz and Killanti had existed since the dawn of time. They had created their cities with space waste; admirably recycling the debris of the universe, but it was what they did with the organic waste that terrified Hamen. The ear pieces he wore to enable his understanding of the guardians were, in fact, harvested from human ears. The guardians existed to learn from and dissect anything that came their way. Nothing was wasted.

"I am her Communer," he said with a tone of authority. "No harm will come to her. I have come to collect her personally."

The guardian nodded. "As a master commands," he said bowing.

Hamen took long strides over to the sleeping Jenni and waved away the greedy eyed guardians who had gathered around her, waiting to take yet another lost soul.

Hamen spoke to rouse the sleeping form of Jenni. His eyes softened as she turned her pale blue gaze towards the sound of his voice.

"This isn't Killanti," she murmured. "Why aren't we by the pool? This looks just like that horrid world with giant mice all over it."

"That's because it is that horrid world with mice all over it," Hamen whispered close to her ear. His could hardly keep the mirth inside him from bubbling up.

Hamen yearned to pull her close and rain kisses down on her, but he knew if he did he wouldn't be able to stop there. He knew he would want more and more of her and did not know if he could stop himself. He didn't know much about the sexual habits of the guardians, but he knew they would not want a floor show of what he had in mind. Jenni was not helping by making small sighing noises and trying to entwine her arms around his neck.

"Wake up!" Hamen's tone was gruff as he tried to rein in his desires.

Jenni eyes started to focus and she gasped as she looked into Hamen's dark shining eyes. "You found me," she smiled. "I knew you would."

Hamen felt a wave of something he had never felt before. It felt like he wanted to gather Jenni up in his strong arms and never let her go again. His need to hold onto her and keep her safe was so overpowering his knees buckled and he sank onto the seat beside her.

"How did you get here?" Hamen asked, bewildered by her presence among the guardians.

"Oh, I hitched a lift," Jenni replied glibly. "I was looking for you."

Hamen let his tongue trace the line of his lips. He wanted to see Jenni aroused; wanted her to want him like he wanted her. He felt a thrill of dominance as Jenni's eyes widened and her pupils grew. He knew she was recalling the pleasure his tongue could evoke in her. Hamen watched intently as Jenni squirmed in her seat. He knew he had made her wet just by showing her a hint of his forked tongue. It wasn't enough to just tease her; he wanted to taste the reaction he just caused and he wanted it now.

"Guardian!" he barked. "Take us to a room where I can question this human. She is almost ready for the knowledge, but I must be sure."

"Through here, master." The guardian opened an old door that looked like it had come from an old Trinz vessel. Inside was a metal counter with a monitor and several colorful buttons, wires and switches protruding from it. Hamen pulled Jenni to her feet and led her in. As soon as he heard the door close behind them, he pulled her into his desperate embrace. Jenni's response was instant. Her need fired the lust in Hamen. He paused only to pull free his own garments before he darted his tongue into the softness of her parted lips.

Jenni's hands closed into his hair and tightened, pulling the roots gently. The sensation ripped through Hamen's body, stopping only when it reached his manhood. He pulsed against her soft body as he relished her touch. Jenni's mew as she felt his need brought Hamen dangerously close to heady abandon. He, too, pulled in vain at the tight clothing, hearing Jenni's low, throaty laugh as she released her grip on his hair and assisted with removing her own clothes.

Naked, they both stood facing each other. They were panting as if they had just reached climax. Jenni was flushed with a color Hamen thought was the most beautiful color he had ever seen. It ran from her cheeks, down her neck then fanned out onto her chest. Hamen decided to explore the trail with his tongue to see how sweet it tasted. Murmuring words of seduction that brought cries of desire from Jenni, he licked his way down her body and right towards the downy hair that heralded her womanly core. Jenni's nub poked cheekily through her swollen lips, and Hamen flicked over it with each side of his arousing tongue. He paused with the nub between each fork then clasped the two sides shut, pushing

Jenni to cry out. Hamen felt her knees buckle and spanned his hands across her rear to steady her. His mouth continued to French kiss her pussy as she ground her hips against him, begging for release with her throaty words.

Hamen's seed begged the same release. He felt alive and filled with power. It was he that had reduced this strong, brave woman to a quivering wreck and he intended to take his prize. Standing up and lifting Jenni effortlessly towards the metal counter, he positioned her on the edge and guided his length into the hot, waiting channel that throbbed for him.

It was so good to enter Jenni and possess her again. Hamen had thought he would never have the chance to love her again.

"I am sorry," Jenni sobbed as her orgasm made her grip him inside her.

"Later," Hamen ground out as he drove into her, marveling at the way she could take hold of him internally. It was like her hand was wrapped around, squeezing gently yet her hands were digging into the flesh of his back as she rubbed her tight nipples against his broad chest.

Unable to hold back his own satisfaction, Hamen thrust deep inside her again and again until he let go with a roar of carnal desire. He felt the eruption of his seed and crowed as he marked her with his life giving liquid.

She's mine! he thought as his mind passed into the blackness that came with giving in to the pure sensation of a moment.

In his arms she trembled. Hamen squeezed her tight as he heard sobs racking through her slim body.

"I am here now," he soothed. "It will be alright. We are together, we can face it all."

"I...I...I..." hiccupped Jenni, "I didn't mean what I said. I didn't want you to go."

"I know, I know! Come on, there is someone I would like you to meet."

With their eyes hardly leaving one another, Jenni and Hamen dressed quickly and left the small room to return to the large area with the mismatched seating. Timon sat there grinning wickedly from ear to ear.

"Lucky bastard!" he drawled, taking in the couple's glow with a sweeping look.

Hamen's glow deepened and he did indeed feel fortunate. "You'll remember Timon," he said, "and this is Cal; my father."

"We've met," said Jenni coolly.

"I owe you an apology, my dear," Cal said, extending his hand. "May we start over?"

Hamen looked expectantly at Jenni. His eyes expressed his desire for peace between these two important people in his life. Seeming to pick up on his silent plea, Jenni nodded and grasped the proffered hand. Hamen smiled as she was pulled into a bear hug by the giant Timon.

"Good to see you, Jen!" he boomed. "Maybe I can ditch this guy and return home to my Hope."

"Masters!" a guardian rushed from the lift and twitched his head between the two Trinz. "There is an unscheduled landing! None should see us here except those who have been chosen. How can it be?"

"I do not know," replied Hamen, "but I can guess who it is. I think maybe our trail was too fresh and it lit up his path here."

"Are he and his companions chosen by The Trinz?" the guardian was practically salivating at the thought of what the reply may be.

"They are not," Hamen shuddered at the implications of his denial.

The guardian emitted a piecing scream even the ear pieces could not filter. Its implication was clear and its insanity shook the small group. Hamen pulled Jenni into his side as he saw her knees buckle.

"What will they do to them?" she asked.

"Best not to think about it," Timon interjected with an attempt at joviality. "Couldn't happen to a nicer guy though."

As the four of them stood still, the earth seemed to shake. The thundering grew louder and louder and the ground vibrated with an unnatural force. From every door, guardians streamed out. Hundreds clamored to get into the lift, scrabbling over each other with a feral intensity. Many others disappeared into what must have been the stairwell and still more came. Within a few minutes, the room cleared and an eerie silence fell over the gathered company. They stood and looked at one another, struck dumb with morbid anticipation. It didn't last though. A guttural scream ripped through the air. Jenni turned into Hamen, taking refuge in the wall of his chest.

Hamen pulled her closer and welcomed the protective instinct that overtook him. It was a small glimmer of something good among the horror unfolding above them.

"Can't we help?" Jenni begged, her quiet tone indicating she already knew the answer to her plea. "I know Lio is evil but he doesn't deserve that."

"It is the way," Timon explained. "They take what cannot make it into Para D.I.S. We know it but rarely experience it firsthand like this."

"How is that the actions of a civilized race?" Jenni was outraged. She pulled away from Hamen and her eyes flashed in anger.

Hamen was caught between shame and arousal. He loved to see the fire in her eyes but knew his race was responsible for the genocide of those not worthy of entering Para D.I.S.

"I think we had better leave," Cal said. "There is a way still to go."

"I will take my leave now that you are reunited with Jenni and the threat of Lio is...well...is over," Timon said.

Hamen realized Timon had voiced what was becoming evident to them all. Without Lio, the threat to Trinz and Killanti was greatly reduced. His stoic determination to find and conquer the whole universe would soon be passed on to another ambitious dictator, Hamen was convinced of it. Although, he would never admit as much to Jenni, he knew that the nature of humankind was varied. Many were open to change and a selfless future but some retained the gene that had led to the devastation of Earth so many years ago.

~ * ~

Jenni knew Lio probably got what he deserved. She knew he would have never given up on his relentless perusal of them. She also knew the sound of the bloodthirsty guardians as they rushed in for the kill would haunt her dreams for a long time to come. As she heard the distant sound of paws on metal returning from their murderous spree, she turned herself back into the warm comfort of Hamen's hard shape. She knew he wasn't to blame for the mistakes of his race any more than she was for hers. Perhaps between them they could strive to make a future that reflected the good in each of their genetics.

Jenni felt the rush of air as door flew open and the hordes of rodents returned to their mundane tasks. The sport was over until the next unsuspecting soul entered Purr Gate.

"Let's go home," she mumbled into Hamen's heat.

The welcome rumble of his chest confirmed his assent.

"I am keen to return to Hope and have no desire to enter the orbit of Trinz again." Timon looked around the assembled group. His companions nodded their assent. They too looked keen to return to the simpler life they had left behind on Jamaica 2.

"I might come with you, if you will have me," Cal spoke to Timon. "This planet you call home sounds like a place I would enjoy."

"I would be honored," Timon bowed.

Brief farewells and promises of future reunions ensued before Timon's ship departed for Jamaica 2 and Hamen secured a small vessel to take Jenni and him the short distance to Trinz.

Chapter Seventeen

As the craft edged closer towards the planet of vivid blue and green, Jenni was filled with a sense of inexplicable peace. Since leaving Purr Gate, Jenni vowed never to return to the place that terrified her more than she could ever express. She knew Hamen sensed a change in her. He had been shooting her concerned looks since their hurried departure two weeks ago. The only option was to continue forward into the Para D.I.S. galaxy with its duel suns and seek out the way to Killanti. Hamen decided to make a detour past Trinz so he could plead for the directions to the elusive place where he knew he could live with Jenni and have the life he now craved to share with her.

Cal had insisted he could reason with Wren. He explained the shame that would be heaped on the Elder and knew he would do anything to avoid that disgrace.

Now that they were headed towards the majestic Trinz, it was Hamen's turn to look nervous. He and Cal had left without the permission of the Elder panel, a crime usually punishable by brain realignment. Hamen knew he would never bow to such a reprimand. He saved Jenni the worry of enlightening her with too much detail of the way crime was dealt with on Trinz. Up until he had seen more of the universe, Haman never questioned the way his people dispensed justice. It had been his norm and therefore, in his inexperienced mind, the way things must be done everywhere.

"Identify yourselves!" came the sharp command. The loud voice filled the small space and made Hamen jolt from his wanderings.

"I am Hamen, son of Rein and of Ju member of the Elder Panel." Hamen did not usually rely on the position of his parents, but, in this case, he knew his name dropping would allow them access to the planet's secure boundaries.

"Wait for instruction," came the slightly less harsh tone of the reply.

"I expect they are calling for verification," Hamen explained, looking to Jenni as he spoke.

Jenni's eyes looked huge in her face and she chewed her lip as if nervous of the forthcoming descent.

"Hamen, is that you?" a feminine voice filled the cabin.

"Mother," Hamen greeted the voice; his own voice filled with delight. "I seek permission to take Jenni to Killanti. I have travelled far to deliver her to the place where she can make a difference. Her soul is pure. May we know the way?"

"She may know the way," the voice seemed to be twinged with regret this time. "You may not."

"No!" Jenni cried out. "I will not be parted from him!"

"It is the way," Rein voiced explained. "The Communer may not pass. Their task is to find more souls. Their part is ongoing."

"But I have been across the universe with Jenni. Our souls met as one and joined. We are destined to be together. I know it."

"I thought the same once too," Rein's voice was now etched with sadness as it spoke, faceless yet with such real emotion.

"I will not be like you!" Hamen grew angry as he pulled himself up in his seat as if he challenged one who was in the space with them. "I demand an audience with the Panel!"

"It is Wren who sent me here," Rein explained. "You must allow us to lock on you then you will be teleported back to the surface whilst Jenni will continue to Killanti. She must arrive alone. I am sorry."

"No!" Jenni and Hamen spoke as one as, for the second time, Hamen's form began to disappear.

Hamen saw Jenni's eyes widen in disbelief as he felt a surge of motion sickness. His body lurched as bright lights flashed before him. Jenni's hand reached out, in vain. He saw her hand grasp nothing as it clenched the space that had once held his physical form.

"I love you!" he heard the words yet saw nothing but blackness.

~ * ~

"I love you," Jenni heard the desperation in her own voice as it repeated the phrase over and over to the empty space that had once held the man she loved. "Come back," she added in a faint whisper.

The silence replied with silence, it resonated around her, eerie in its nothingness. Jenni sat, unsure of what to do next. The voice of what had been Hamen's mother had indicated she would be told the way. Jenni fumed. She would not be told the way. She would no longer be told what to do. She wanted to be with Hamen so she would find her way to him instead.

Jenni laid her hands on the touch screen. She ran her fingers over the navigational keys in vain. There was no response. Jenni drew shapes over the surface, trying to elicit a response from the ship. She was determined to take over control of her own destiny. The ship, it seemed, had other ideas. It fired to life and shot across the starless expanse of space, leaving the planet in its wake. Jenni felt her head spinning as the craft flashed through the inky blackness. Overwhelmed by the intense sensation of speed, Jenni lost consciousness. Her head lolled against the seat and her mind went as black at the space she traversed.

~ * ~

Waking up, Jenni's first sensation was the smell. The mustiness of the craft had been replaced by the fresh zest of foliage. Jenni forced her eyes to embrace the brightness that filtered through her closed lids. Duel suns beamed down from a cloudless sky hued with a pink glow. Jenni became aware of overhanging branches and a soft grassy bed beneath her. She allowed her fingers to sink into the cool blades, feeling the moist dewy sensation of morning on each tip. Her eyes left the perfect sky and travelled, knowingly instinctively, what she would behold. The pool lay to her left; tranquil as if inviting her to partake of its luxuriating waters. As if hypnotized, Jenni stood and walked towards the familiar ripples as a leaf fluttered from its lofty home to settle on the surface. Shedding her clothes as she walked, Jenni arrived at the edge naked and stepped in. The rocks lay bathed in sunlight, ready for her to climb and stretch out in the warmth of the day. Jenni submerged her body and tossed her head back into the chilly depths of the pool.

Lost in her own delight, Jenni rubbed her scalp and felt the tension leaving her. Lifting her legs from the sandy bed, she floated under the rosy sky and sighed. A smile spread slowly over her face.

He's here.

Every nerve in her body knew him; knew he was there. He was there just as he always had been; just as he had been from the start.

"What kept you?" she asked shyly, at once aware of her nakedness.

"I was waiting for you to arrive," he caressed her with his voice, sending goose bumps across her body.

"I'm here," she replied. "Come to me."

A gentle splash followed. Jenni struggled to contain the shiver of anticipation that convulsed through her body. She knew he was close yet it seemed an age before two strong hands fastened around her waist and pulled her to him. His chest was bare and his warmth radiated through the cool water.

"Is this a dream?" Jenni asked, dreading the truth of his reply.

"We are here, together, at last," he breathed into her ear as she turned her head and met his lips.

Their kiss; the kiss of true love, united them as one under the rose-colored skies of Killanti.

About the Author

lorettalairdx@hotmail.com

My name is Loretta Laird and I am a romanceaholic! I love to get lost in a book though seldom get the opportunity being a busy mum to four daughters! I moved from England to Australia in 2009 and love the lifestyle here. I enjoy cooking, mostly cakes as that's what I love to eat. My ambition is to buy a cabin by a lake and sit and write all day, creating worlds and stories that are enjoyed by many.

www.ingramcontent.com/pod-product-compliance
Lightning Source LLC
Chambersburg PA
CBHW060435130626
46555CB00005B/2360